Beyond the Textbook

Beyond the Textbook

Using Trade Books and Databases to Teach Our Nation's History, Grades 7–12

Carianne Bernadowski, Robert Del Greco, and Patricia L. Kolencik

LIBRARIES UNLIMITED

AN IMPRINT OF ABC-CLIO, LLC
Santa Barbara, California • Denver, Colorado • Oxford, England

Library of Congress Cataloging-in-Publication Data

Bernadowski, Carianne.
  Beyond the textbook : using trade books and databases to teach our nation's history, grades 7-12 / Carianne Bernadowski, Robert Del Greco, and Patricia L. Kolencik.
     p. cm.
  Includes bibliographical references and index.
    ISBN 978-1-61069-037-9 (hardcopy : alk. paper) — ISBN 978-1-61069-038-6 (ebook) 1. United States—History—Study and teaching. 2. Young adult literature, American. 3. Historical fiction, American. I. Greco, Robert Del. II. Kolencik, Patricia Liotta. III. Title.
  E175.8.B47   2013
  973.071—dc23   2012041475

ISBN: 978-1-61069-037-9
EISBN: 978-1-61069-038-6

17 16 15 14 13   1 2 3 4 5

This book is also available on the World Wide Web as an eBook.
Visit www.abc-clio.com for details.

Libraries Unlimited
An Imprint of ABC-CLIO, LLC

ABC-CLIO, LLC
130 Cremona Drive, P.O. Box 1911
Santa Barbara, California 93116-1911

This book is printed on acid-free paper ∞

Manufactured in the United States of America

Dedicated to my boys, Maxwell and Liam

—*Carianne Bernadowski*

Dedicated to my loving husband, Tony

—*Patricia Kolencik*

Dedicated to my wife, Pat, and our children, Jay, Ryan,
and Mari

—*Robert Del Greco*

Contents

Illustrations

Introduction

WE ARE ALL TEACHERS OF LITERACY

Literacy. Simply put, it is the ability to read, write, and comprehend words. When the concept of "being literate" arose years ago, it referred to those few individuals who were considered to be "educated" because they were able to read and write. Today, the new ethos of the term *literacy* embraces a number of specialized literacies, such as information literacy, visual literacy, media literacy, digital literacy, and so on, all of which require the ability and skills to read, write, and/or understand symbols or pictures. Regardless of your discipline, we are all teachers of literacy.

Literacy is the spine that holds everything together in all subject areas. The branches of learning connect to it, meaning that all core content teachers have a responsibility to teach literacy (Phillips and Wong). Although the primary responsibility for addressing literacy instruction lies with the classroom teacher, the librarian also plays an important role in supporting literacy development. An important contribution for the library program is to provide access to a wide variety of quality literature that teachers can use within the library setting or in their classroom collections. Library media specialists, who are literature experts, are valuable resources for the classroom teacher because they have expertise in selecting materials that have substance, style, rich language, and themes relevant to today's adolescents. They can offer assistance to the classroom teacher in developing quality thematic units and can suggest aspects of literary response. Through this collaborative effort, both the social studies teacher and the librarian share the responsibility of providing each student with meaningful experiences commensurate with the needs of the student not only as a learner, but also as a human being and a productive citizen. Thus, we all share a joint responsibility for integrating literacy skills into the curriculum regardless of the content area.

We don't need to think outside the box when we discuss literacy instruction and learning and its curricular integration. We need to think inside the box, inside the classrooms in which we teach daily. We need to examine what we teach and how we teach. Research has shown that what we teach, how we teach, and the amount of time we spend teaching it account for the greatest variance in student achievement (Strickland and Alvermann). Therefore, as educators, we need to scrutinize our instructional strategies and the materials, especially the books, that we use in our daily core practice to enhance and strengthen our literacy instruction. We need to create and to fashion our teaching strategies to fit the needs of our students by combining the best approaches to both literacy and social studies instruction.

Standards provide us with a framework and provide clear, concrete teaching goals. However, we all know that standards as well as assessments alone do not make for effective teaching. It is the teacher's powerful ways to intertwine lasting and meaningful memories for reading and writing with the core content that will make the difference in the classroom. In sum, what we teach and how we teach in any discipline, especially in social studies, are inseparable from the teaching of literacy—from the integration of purposeful and meaningful reading and writing to engage students in constructing knowledge. Wineburg and Martin said it best: "Literacy is the key word here, because the teaching of history should have reading and writing at its core" (42).

The incorporation of literacy skills into every lesson will have a game-changing impact on student engagement, retention, and lifelong learning. Literacy demands on our society have increased exponentially as we have progressed from the Industrial Age to the Digital Age. In their book *Content Area Reading: Literacy and Learning across the Curriculum*, Vacca, Vacca, and Mrza state that "adolescents entering the adult world of the 21st century will read and write more than any other time in human history. Students will need advanced levels of literacy to perform their jobs, run their households, act as citizens, and conduct their personal lives. They will need literacy to cope with the flood of information they will find everywhere they turn. Students will need literacy to feed their imagination so they can create the world of the future" (38). Even with the explosion of technology, reading and writing with independence and confidence will remain master arts in the information age (Phillips and Wong). Thus, in order to break the glass ceiling and enable all students to succeed and to read—to write and to communicate effectively at every level—all teachers must be teachers of literacy.

In sum, let us ask the essential question: How important is it that we all be teachers of literacy? Hirsch argues that "verbal competency [literacy] is the most important single goal of schooling in any nation" (31). Schmoker concludes that literacy is foundational to learning in every subject. Social studies and literacy are mutually dependent on each other. When literacy skills are taught in the context of social studies content, students are able to recognize the value and purpose of the skills. Moreover, they are able to apply the skills in a meaningful context using real-world information and resources. Thus, we all must be teachers of literacy.

ENHANCING CURRICULUM WITH HISTORICAL FICTION

"This history textbook is so boring."
"Why do we have to memorize all these battles and dates?"
"Who cares about the Battle of Waterloo!"

Do these student remarks sound familiar? These student comments make a good case to enhance the social studies curriculum by integrating literature, specifically, historical fiction, in social studies teaching. The textbook, despite continuing improvements in visual appeal, no longer needs to be the foundation for teaching American history.

Because students tend to find the information in textbooks boring, one needs to consider bringing history "alive" by integrating historical fiction. If the only thing a teacher shares is from a textbook, how are we going to get students excited about learning—and reading for that matter? Study after study has concluded that today's graduates of American high schools have little knowledge and less understanding of their country's past. Although students "occupy" seats in American history class, trudge through their history textbooks, and generally pass the tests, they have not learned very much. They have crammed "facts" to get through the exam. But when the exam is over, all is forgotten. That is because students have not been actively engaged in learning social studies concepts through knowledge construction.

WHAT IS HISTORICAL FICTION?

According to the *Encyclopedia Britannica*, historical fiction, also referred to as historical novels, "has as its setting a period of history and . . . attempts to convey the spirit, manners, and social conditions of a past age with realistic detail and fidelity (which is in some cases only apparent fidelity) to historical fact." The Historical Novel Society further qualifies this definition in the following way: "To be deemed historical, a novel must have been written at least fifty years after the events described, or have been written by someone who was not alive at the time of those events and who therefore approaches them only by research." According to the definition, novels like Sir Walter Scott's *Ivanhoe*, Dickens's *A Tale of Two Cities*, Fenimore Cooper's *The Last of the Mohicans*, Hawthorne's *The Scarlet Letter*, or Kantor's *Andersonville* would be considered historical fiction because they were written about a time period in which the author did not live. Austen's *Pride and Prejudice* or Hemingway's *A Farewell to Arms* would not be considered historical fiction because these novels were written by authors about their own time periods.

The purpose of historical fiction is to give today's reader a glimpse of a time period far distant from their own. An author may do this in several ways: (1) by dramatizing the impact of a public event of the historical time, (2) by taking a position on a historical controversy involving people who actually lived during that time period, (3) by fictionalizing the biography of a real person from that time period, or (4) by portraying fictional characters involved in real events. At times, the author may be painstakingly accurate in his or her portrayal of the time period, or the details in the book may give you only the vaguest feeling of the era.

Types of Historical Fiction

Historical fiction is written in two styles. One style uses fictional persons and does not distinguish any specific occurrence in history. The other style describes authentic people and incidents where the author represents the time period precisely and accurately concerning dress, speech, and other styles during a particular historical period.

Some guided reading questions that the teacher and librarian need to consider when selecting a historical fiction work to encourage students' critical thinking skills with regard to the content to be studied would be:

1. Was the story realistic?
2. Were the characters fictional or actual people?
3. Did the story accurately represent the time period?
4. How does the story hold the reader's attention differently than the textbook?
5. Will reading this story allow the student to better understand the time period and the historical and cultural heritage?
6. Did this story show how people of the past solved problems and handled mistakes?

Why Should Historical Fiction Be Used within the Social Studies Curriculum?

Historical fiction can be the antidote to combat the widespread disinterest in and lack of excitement about the study of American history. Simply speaking, historical fiction consists of realistic tales that have been set in the past. Yet historical fiction has the power to revitalize and inspire students' interest in studying and learning history. Integrating historical fiction with the textbook provides the opportunity to heighten student interest, stimulate imagination, provoke creativity, deepen understanding and critical thinking, create moods and atmosphere, portray the diverse ways of living and thinking among people in various cultures, promote empathy, build appreciation for the contributions of others, and provide vivid, realistic impressions of people and their ways of living. By reading historical fiction, students may come to see history as the story of "real" people with feelings, values, and needs to which they themselves can relate, based on their own experiences and interests. Students will discover that the key actors in the story are ordinary people doing, for the most part, what ordinary people do and feeling like ordinary people feel. This feeling of connection, of participation in the story, is critical for students to develop increased comprehension of their country's past. When students begin to see history "as a story" featuring ordinary people like themselves instead of a "bunch of facts and dates," they can develop that critical spirit of inquiry so important to a real understanding of historical events because both cognitive and affective processes are activated. The hard data in the textbook will have more meaning after students are plunged vicariously into the experiences of fictional young people building a sod house or parachuting into enemy territory. These vicarious experiences will truly help students acquire understanding of people in different times and places. More important, these vicarious experiences from reading strengthen their literacy skills.

Historical fiction helps students to experience and understand other people, times, and situations. Learning through stories is a natural way to learn. Throughout history, humans have used stories, myths, and legends to carry important ideas from one generation to another (Campbell). Historical fiction stories are far more interesting than lists of dates and facts. Cognitively speaking, the mind can absorb and remember stories more easily because the story line often draws things together in a logical sequence. Additionally, students are able to connect to the stories more easily because the stories elicit both personal and emotional experiences from which they can draw. This connection enables students to make associations to their own lives. Throughout the stories, facts and concepts become more relevant, and students are able to become more engaged and think at a deeper level about the concepts.

Rosenblatt indicates that reading literature such as historical fiction makes known the many ways that humans meet life's possibilities. Reading books and hearing stories allows students to hear the thoughts of others and make contact with other values, dreams, and philosophies.

Historical fiction can enhance students' ability to engage in moral reasoning and can assist students in clarifying their own values. The thoughts of literary characters struggling with issues and situations can be used to teach character education by exposing students to the value and moral reasoning of others who are searching for what they consider to be the best action or behavior in a given circumstance. Exposure to literary characters who work out their principles and values creates the conditions in which students can reflect upon and gain perspective on their own. Additionally, the problems and situations faced by the characters in the story can be used as problem-solving and moral-reasoning activities for students.

Finally, integrating historical fiction can also assist students in making sound choices. When students have the opportunity to read historical fiction, they may encounter the imaginary trials and errors of others. Students can vicariously experience the logical consequences of certain actions without having to experience the actual experiences or consequences. Historical fiction may help students view their own problems or situations more objectively. For example, if a student is going through an abusive situation, reading about the abusive situation of another may provide a context for that student to make sense of the situation and may offer some ideas regarding a possible course of action. Similarly, if students are making decisions regarding drugs, alcohol, sex, gangs, or crime, experiencing the full impact of possible decisions through the actions of some literary characters may help to provide insight. In sum, historical fiction provides a history lesson in fictional form where students can read about historical figures and see them come alive.

The bottom line in enhancing any social studies curriculum is to keep in mind the purpose of teaching and learning—to get students to think critically. Teachers and school librarians can enhance student understanding of social studies through the effective use of literature, specifically historical fiction. According to Gerwin and Zevin, "we want to hear their ideas; we want to see evidence, and above all we want to hear reasons, hypotheses and interpretations that analyze and explain events" (68). Levstik and Barton describe a classroom in which students are "doing history" (39). What better way to do this than to integrate historical fiction into the curriculum?

INTEGRATING RESEARCH-BASED INSTRUCTIONAL STRATEGIES INTO THE SOCIAL STUDIES CURRICULUM

This section describes a variety of research-based reading strategies and activities that can be used in daily practice to develop both literacy and social studies skills through the use of historical fiction. The strategies and activities are all designed to get students to interact with story ideas and to make personal connections with the literature, which will in turn enhance the literacy skills of reading, writing, and comprehension, as well as social studies content skills. Additionally, these strategies and activities can also be the basis for literature log entries and other types of assignments. It is critical to always keep the following guiding principle in mind when selecting a strategy: students learn best when they are able to connect it to something they already know. Savage et al. state that one problem students face is not "recognizing the relevance" of background experiences (22). Teachers and school librarians need to assist students in identifying the connection between prior knowledge and the academic task at hand. When content is presented in a way that connects to the lives of students, they will remember it and be able to incorporate new knowledge and apply that knowledge to learn more. In other words, activating students' prior knowledge is essential.

1. Previewing the Text

Before reading, ask students to consider the following questions:

1. What is the *P*urpose of the reading?
2. What are the *I*mportant ideas?
3. What *C*onnections can they make?

This learning strategy is known as PIC. PIC can be used to help students develop good reading habits by encouraging them to spend a few minutes organizing their thinking and setting their goals *before* beginning an assignment. This strategy enables students to set a purpose for their reading, identify the most important ideas, and connect what they already know from the text to their experience and prior knowledge. Often when students read, they do not think about what is really important to remember. Previewing reading assignments helps students focus on the most important information and effectively facilitates storing information in long-term memory, which makes for better context for comprehension. Additionally, you may ask students to skim the structure of the text for main ideas and think about what they will be expected to do with the reading—such as write a report, explain a concept to a peer, apply the information in a different setting, or take a test. It also would be feasible to ask students to make a prediction after they identify the main ideas.

After students have read the text, encourage them to go back to their PIC preview and see if their questions were answered. After reading, they can confirm that their predictions were correct, or they may want to change what they thought were the text's main ideas. Additionally, you can add an after-reading component by asking students to discuss the questions they wanted answered in a small group or class discussion setting.

2. Content Information, Sequencing, and Signal Words

In order for students to understand the series of events that led up to, for example, the Civil War, sequencing and signal words are essential. Thinking about the chronology of events is critical to the study of history.

Signal words usually indicate the text's structure. When students are attuned to cue words such as *first*, *second*, *before*, *during*, *then*, or *finally*, they are able to organize information, a skill critical to learning. Other signal words, such as *for example* or *for instance*, indicate that examples or descriptions will follow. Words such as *because*, *since*, or *consequently* indicate a cause and effect relationship. Words such as *different*, *as opposed to*, *instead of*, or *although* indicate a compare and contrast correlation.

When students play an active role in ordering information that they have been studying, their ability to sequence contributes to the understanding of social studies concepts. Ask students to list the main ideas by creating an outline, writing a summary, or creating a concept map that integrates the chronology of the event. It is the organization, that is, sequencing of information, along with the signal words that indicate structure and help students understand, remember, and use the major concepts presented in the text.

3. Graphic Organizers

Graphic organizers—visual representations that help students organize, study, and remember material—are essential active learning tools for teaching social studies concepts. Sometimes called semantic maps or concept maps, graphic organizers are especially useful to "help activate student learning when used with social studies textbooks," and they "are also very appropriate for use with nonfiction informational books" (Kuhrt and Farris 136). Graphic organizers can be used to demonstrate students' competence in metacognitive skills and other performance-based standards. Graphic organizers; diagrams; charts; and maps composed of lines, arrows, boxes, and so on support students' learning, helping them understand content by showing relationships. The graphic organizers assist students by making abstract ideas more concrete. These graphical representations, sometimes called semantic maps or webs, enable students to classify information and organize their thinking, knowledge, concepts, or ideas in a visual format. They help students visualize the connections between and among ideas as well as make to connections to what they already know. They help students make sense of disjointed facts and information. Indrisano and Paratore indicate that graphic organizers help readers focus attention on, organize, and recall their reading of expository text (146). Additionally, graphic organizers can also be used as a stimulus for writing.

Graphic organizers should first be used for whole-class instruction with a variety of social studies topics. Teachers should then design activities and assignments in which students use graphic organizers in small cooperative learning groups, in pairs, and in individual assignments. For students who struggle and may need additional support, you can create a cloze concept map, that is, an almost completed graphic organizer where some of the boxes are left blank. If you think students may have difficulty completing this cloze concept map, a word bank can be provided.

Examples of graphic organizers and templates for student use are available online at different websites, such as the North Central Regional laboratory site (http://www.ncrel.org/sdrs/areas/issues/students/learning/lr1grorg.htm). Software such as Inspiration (http://www.inspiration.com) and Kidspiration (http://www.inspiration.com/Kidspiration) has also been developed to allow teacher and students to create visual organizers. This type of software enables teachers and students to enter information into a variety of graphic organizers and to manipulate the information in an interactive format.

The way that ideas are presented in a text dictates what type of thinking is necessary to understand and remember those ideas. Therefore, graphic organizers can be divided into four types: (1) cause and effect, (2) problem and solution, (3) compare and contrast, and (4) sequence or chronological order. Cause and effect graphic organizers are used to show the causal interaction of a complex event, for example, a national election or a complex phenomenon such as drug trafficking. Key questions are: What are the factors that cause X? How do they interrelate? Are the factors that cause X the same as those that cause X to persist? Figure I.1 is an example of a cause and effect organizer where students identify the cause and effect relationships between an event (cause: rising gas prices) and existing conditions (effects) and then attempt to discover the relationship between the current event and future conditions. Using Figure I.1 students would be asked to list the effects that rising gas prices will have on transportation costs, travel, farming, and the price of groceries and other goods that are transported by truck. This is done in the left column. In the right column, students would be asked to list or describe how these effects might impact future conditions. For example, higher gas prices might result in less travel, more fuel-efficient vehicles, or more government money given for research and development of alternative fuels.

Problem and solution graphic organizers are used to represent a problem, for example, the national debt, along with attempted solutions and results. Key questions are: What was the problem? Who had the problem? Why was it a problem? What attempts were made to solve the problem? Did the attempts succeed? Figures I.2, I.3, and I.4 illustrate several versions of problem and solution graphic organizers. These organizers can be used to have students work individually, with a partner, or in groups.

Cause and Effect Organizer

Cause: Rising gas prices	
Effects	**Future Conditions**
Interesting or important ideas:	

Figure I.1: Cause and Effect Organizer

Problem and Solution Graphic Organizer

Problem Analysis	
What was the problem?	
Who had the problem?	
Why was it a problem?	

Solution	
What attempts were made to solve the problem? 1. 2.	What were the results? Did the attempt succeed?
End Results	

Figure I.2: Problem and Solution Graphic Organizer

Problem and Solution Graphic Organizer

Problem:	
Important background information:	
Ideas:	Initial solution/plan:
	Elaborate and refine:
	Final solution:

Figure I.3: Problem and Solution Graphic Organizer

Problem and Solution Graphic Organizer: Examining Solutions

Problem:

Solutions	Positive Consequences	Negative Consequences

Decision:

Supporting Statements:

1.

2.

3.

Figure I.4: Problem and Solution Graphic Organizer: Examining Solutions

Compare and contrast graphic organizers are used to show similarities and differences between two things, people, places, events, ideas, or concepts. Key questions are: What things are being compared? How are they similar? How are they different? Sequence or chronological graphic organizers are used to describe stages of a linear procedure or a series or sequence of events, such as how feudalism led to the formation of nation states, or the goals, actions, and outcomes of a historical figure or character in a novel, or the rise and fall of Hitler. Figure I.5, Compare and Contrast Graphic Organizer, is an example of sequential organization of information. Key questions include: What is the object, procedure, or initiating event? What are the stages or steps? How do they lead to one another? What is the final outcome?

4. Predicting and Confirming Activity (PACA)

Students may feel frustrated and overwhelmed as they attempt to read their social studies textbook or other resources because they know very little about the topics at hand. The predicting and confirming activity (PACA) can help students build the background information they need to be successful before beginning a reading assignment. PACA is based on Beyer's inquiry model. The purpose of this strategy is to help build background information when students are going to read about something they know very little about so that when they approach the reading selection, they will be more successful and have a context for understanding the

Compare and Contrast Graphic Organizer

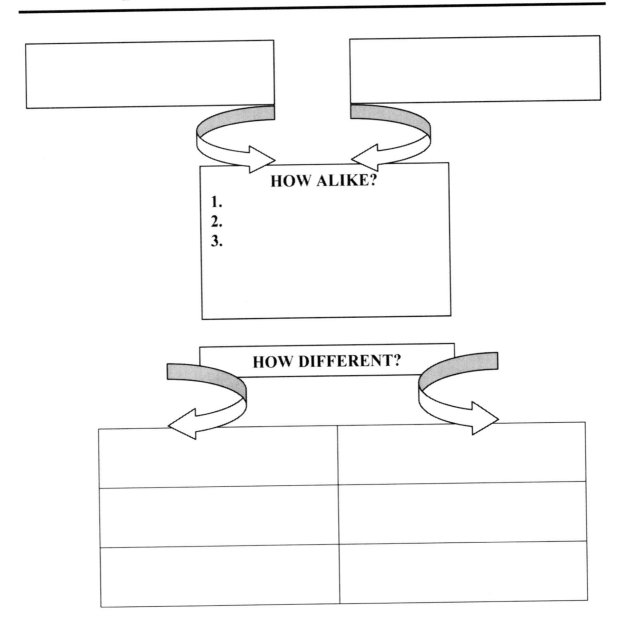

Figure I.5: Compare and Contrast Graphic Organizer

information, ideas, or concepts it presents. Students often have no personal connection with much of what we hope they will learn in the social studies classroom, but this activity helps students make connections between the new information and what they already know.

The predicting and confirming activity uses student predictions to set a purpose for reading. This activity allows students to analyze the background information and activate their prior knowledge. Students make these predictions based on initial information provided by the teacher. The following steps outline the procedure for the PACA:

1. The teacher or school librarian provides some initial information and poses a general question. Generally speaking, a question or two is usually enough to assist the students in making predictions. The classroom teacher or school librarian may also provide a word list composed of new vocabulary that is relevant to the content.
2. Students write predictions about the text based on the initial information.
3. The teacher provides students with new information.
4. The class reviews student predictions and turns them into questions.
5. Students read the text.
6. Students look back at their predictions and answer the questions generated earlier.

5. Anticipation Guide

Anticipating what a text is going to be about helps students connect the ideas in the text with their experiences and what they already know about a topic. The anticipation guide is an active prereading strategy used to activate prior knowledge and preconceptions about a topic before the students begin reading the text, as well as to provide reinforcement of key concepts after reading. This strategy is well suited for teaching social studies content and helps students clarify their ideas and voice their opinions about a topic. The anticipation guide, which is similar to the PACA in that it asks students to make predictions, provides a structure for discussing ideas and affords an opportunity to expand student thinking. Figure I.6 is an example of an anticipation guide for use in the classroom or library.

Developed by Readence, Bean, and Baldwin, this strategy is most useful with expository texts but may also be used with narrative texts. Anticipation guides are valuable for several reasons: (1) to activate students' prior knowledge, (2) to stimulate class discussion, (3) to develop critical thinking skills, and (4) to promote cross-cultural understanding.

The anticipation guide consists of a list of statements related to the text students will be reading. The teacher prepares four to six clear statements that reflect key concepts in the content that students are expected to learn. These statements should challenge students' preconceptions and may include some true and false statements. Statements should not be generalizations or abstract in nature. Students will then respond to each statement before reading and defend their beliefs and opinions. (See the template in Figure I.7, the Anticipation Guide Template.) After students have responded to each statement, the teacher should plan to conduct open, whole-class, or small group discussion. Note any recurring themes in the discussion, as well as any opposing points of view. At this point, the teacher should clarify a purpose for reading so that students see the connection between the anticipation guide and the required reading. Students are then directed to read the text either silently or orally and look for ideas that support or contradict the statements. After reading, students respond to each statement under the postreading section. To conclude this activity, students should compare their

Anticipation Guide Example

Directions: In the column titled "Before Reading," write A for agree or D for disagree after reading each statement. Do the same in the "After Reading" column upon completion of reading and class discussion.

Before Reading A=Agree D=Disagree	Topic: Shakespeare	After Reading
	Romeo and Juliet is considered a tragedy because of the protagonists in the story.	
	Queen Mab is a well-known queen that Shakespeare introduced to literature in his first play, *Othello*.	
	The Cobbe portrait is considered to be the only authentic image of Shakespeare made during his lifetime.	
	Twelfth Night was first performed in 1604 at a law school in London.	
	As You Like It was the first comedy written by Shakespeare.	

Figure I.6: Anticipation Guide Example

before-reading reactions to their after-reading reactions. Engage students in a summary discussion in which they justify their new or continuing beliefs based on the reading.

6. Questioning the Author (QtA)

Questioning the Author (QtA) is an active reading strategy that employs the question to increase student engagement with text at varying levels. Beck et al. ("Questioning") developed Questioning the Author (QtA) to help students become actively involved in reading text *during* the reading process. This technique teaches students to "question" the authors' intentions, purpose, and authority when reading. Unique to QtA is the idea that textbook authors are not all-knowing but fallible and capable of unintentionally or sometimes intentionally misinforming readers. By teaching students to question the author's credibility, this strategy can increase students' critical thinking skills. The teacher should make it clear to students that any author can potentially be fallible. Letting students know that the content presented is someone's ideas, that the author is a person who sometimes makes mistakes, will provide students the opportunity to understand they have the right to question the author.

Ultimately, QtA consists of four components to assist students in comprehension of text: (a) it addresses text as the product of a fallible author, (b) it deals with text through general

Anticipation Guide Template

Directions: Respond to each statement before reading. Respond to each statement after reading.

Prereading		Statement	Postreading	
Agree	Disagree		Agree	Disagree

Figure I.7: Anticipation Guide Template

probes for meaning directed toward making sense of ideas in the text, (c) it takes place in the context of reading as it initially occurs, and (d) it encourages collaboration in the construction of meaning (Beck et al., "Questioning" 387).

The QtA strategy has three main components: planning the implementation, creating queries, and developing discussions. Before using the strategy prepare students by informing them that they will be learning a new way of reading and dealing with text. Be sure to advise students that a new way of reading text will take time, patience, and practice, so they should not expect immediate results.

The first step is the planning process. Here, the teacher critically reads the text and identifies any major concepts that students must take away from the text while anticipating any problems that readers may encounter. Next, the teacher must segment the text by determining where to stop reading in order to initiate the query that will develop into a discussion. It is important to note that the text should be segmented where understanding should occur or where confusion may occur. It is not necessary to stop at the end of paragraphs or sections.

The second step is the creation and development of "queries" by the teacher. Queries are designed to invite "understanding, interpretation, and elaboration by having students explore the meaning of what is written in the texts they read" (Beck et al., *Questioning* 387). Queries are a vital part of the QtA process and differ significantly from questions. Questions are usually used to assess students' comprehension of text, evaluate individual student responses, and prompt teacher-to-student interactions, either before or after reading. Queries, on the other hand, assist students in grappling with text ideas to construct meaning, facilitate group discussions, and are used during initial reading (Beck et al., *Questioning*). Questions have traditionally been teacher initiated, while queries serve as the focal point of the lesson or interaction with text. Queries allow the librarian or classroom teacher to be a facilitator of the discussion in the library or classroom. There are three types of queries to be used during the reading: initiating, follow-up, and narrative. Initiating queries include: What is the author trying to say? What is the author's message? What is the author talking about?

The second type of query, the follow-up, helps students look at "what the text *means* rather than what the text *says*" (Beck et al., *Questioning* 387). Examples of follow-up prompts include: What does the author mean? Does the author explain this clearly? Does this make sense with knowing what the author told us previously? Why do you think the author tells us this now?

The third type of query is used specifically with narrative text. These queries differ significantly from the queries used with expository text since the structure and nature of text differ in a story. Queries used for narrative text may deal with story structure, characters, and/or plot development. Examples of such queries may include: How do things look for this character now? How has the author let you know that something has changed? Does that change make sense given what we know about the character(s)?

The final step in the QtA process is the discussion element. It is the job of the students to construct meaning from the text. The teacher should spend little time explaining text to students. Instead, students should be grappling with text and dealing with the uncertainty of the text, with guidance from teacher. The teacher should repeat the queries for each segment or section of text.

7. Reading Response Log

The reading response log is an active writing tool that provides an opportunity for students to demonstrate their learning and understanding of the content. It also provides an avenue for clarifying students' thought processes. The reading response log format is composed of two parts. The first part of the log is where students must summarize their reading in four to six sentences. Here they are simply retelling what they have read. The second part of the log is the student's response, which should be a minimum of 12–15 sentences. The response is the student's reaction to and reflection on the reading, in which he or she can share his or her thinking. Possible ways to begin a response are: (1) This connects to my life in this way . . . , (2) I wonder . . . , (3) This is important because. . . . (4) I don't understand . . . because. . . . (5) I would like to learn more about . . . because . . . , and so on. Students may also quote a passage and then respond to it. The response should be the most interesting and informative part of the reading log. It is through the response section that the teacher will be able to assess student learning.

8. Reciprocal Teaching

Reciprocal Teaching is an interactive questioning strategy in which students collaborate to understand a selection of content. This strategy encourages students to ask informed questions and promotes independent learning from a text through inquiry. It teaches four strategies: prediction, summarization, questioning, and clarification. This activity is done in a small group setting and is effective for generating personal interaction. Based on the work of Palincsar and Brown, Reciprocal Teaching is designed to have students "take on" the role of the teacher by generating questions from their reading. It provides a simple introduction to group discussion techniques aimed at understanding, remembering, and analyzing text content through questioning. Reciprocal Teaching is a highly structured metacognitive method that incorporates a number of literacy skills—listening, writing, reading, and speaking. Thus, Reciprocal Teaching is a technique used to develop comprehension of expository text in which both the teacher and the students take turns leading a dialogue concerning sections of a text. Using this strategy, students and teachers establish a dialogue and work together in comprehending text; thus, the result is deep analysis of the reading selection to improve comprehension. Within the group, students take on roles as a summarizer, a questioner, a clarifier, or a predictor. One student is chosen to lead the discussion of each section of the text that was read. Students take turns leading the discussion. The discussion leader asks questions, and the rest of the group responds. Additional questions can be raised by any member of the group. If anything is unclear, the clarifier asks for discussion to address the problem areas. The group also checks if their earlier predictions were accurate. Finally, the summarizer gives the summary with additional comments from the other members of the group. The teacher monitors what is happening in the groups and notes any changes that have to be made to help students read with comprehension. The fact that students learn to develop their own questions about the reading selection is advantageous in enhancing reading comprehension.

USING TECHNOLOGY FOR INSTRUCTIONAL PURPOSES

A quality social studies program in cooperation with a quality school library program ensures that each student has access to necessary technology tools and that they can use these tools effectively. Technology tools enable students to access information and provide them with teaching and learning tools that may not be available in an alternate format. Social studies teachers can use technology to promote specific instructional objectives by creating authentic experiences that encourage critical and active student learning. The National Council for the Social Studies (NCSS) has developed guidelines for using technology in social studies. The guidelines, drawn from the National Educational Technology Standards (NETS), are organized in five categories. Understanding the standards is an important step in determining how technology can effectively be integrated within the social studies curriculum. Each of the guidelines focuses on a different aspect of technology integration, including teacher knowledge, planning and teaching, assessing, and ethics. When planning for using technology, the NCSS Technology Guidelines suggest that teachers should "design developmentally appropriate learning opportunities that apply technology-enhanced instructional strategies to support the diverse needs of learners." Perhaps more than any other area, developmental issues must be considered when integrating technology into social studies. Technology offers special opportunities, but it also creates unique challenges. Before making the decision to use technology to enhance the instruction of your social studies classes, keep in mind that there is no "magic" technology solution to fit every class. Moreover, there are multiple factors to consider before making technology a principal aspect of a classroom lesson. Teachers should consult with the library media specialist to (1) match the technology to the students, (2) match the technology to the content, and (3) match the technology to the teaching methods.

To help determine whether the technology is a good match for students, think about the following factors: (1) consider students' manual dexterity, visual acuity, auditory skills, and ability to incorporate images and sounds as abstractions into learning; (2) consider students' emotional maturity; (3) consider students' language and linguistic abilities; and (4) consider students' learning styles. If students are at different levels and have different abilities, consider how long it will take to bring students up to the skill level they will need in order to complete the activity.

To help determine whether the technology is a good match for the content of the lesson, think about the following questions: (1) Will visual enhancements such as video add to or detract from the message? (2) Will learning be enhanced by communication and collaboration such as email, epals, or e-experts? (3) Can technology reinforce learning in a unique way, such as with digital role playing? and (4) Is the content something that can be segmented into discrete parts or ideas using a technology such as PowerPoint?

To help determine whether the technology is a good match to the teaching methodology, think about the following factors: (1) For the whole class, is the use of a digital projector the best way to deliver content? (2) For small group work and peer collaboration, can students effectively develop presentations, web pages, or other electronic assignments? (3) For individual instruction, can students effectively use an integrated learning system? (4) How many computers or other technological devices will be needed for the activity, and how reliable is the hardware? (5) How much time is required to use the specific technology, and to what extent will specific technological skills be required for the activity? (6) Will students be able to focus on the social studies subject matter when using the technology without distraction?

In sum, the integration of technology into the social studies curriculum is a good choice when it meets the specific needs of students and enhances content and methodology.

Using Databases for Instructional Purposes

Today's students are not satisfied with the lecture method of teaching and the simple memorization of facts and dates. Using databases offers another instructional resource that can be attractive to students. Real-life simulations using databases create a realistic and fun educational activity. Students are naturally attracted to computers, so searching databases is an exciting tool that students can use not only to find facts but also to analyze and evaluate those facts.

The vastness of internet resources can be overwhelming. Finding resources on the web can be like looking for the proverbial needle in a haystack. Both teachers and students must exercise care when trying to find meaningful resources. Online databases offer an excellent alternative resource. They provide access to primary sources such as magazine articles; newspapers; and journals by title, subject, author, and many other access points.

Databases can be used as cognitive tools to greatly enhance the social studies classroom, keeping social studies education dynamic and relevant and helping students make real-world connections. Databases enable students to manipulate information and conduct authentic social studies research. Database searching helps students begin to gain organizational skills that will help them in research, note taking, and writing. Learning to sort and filter data on a database will help students understand how data can be narrowed down to a certain topic. For example, if a student wanted information about George Washington, the keyword entered might be "Washington." Obviously, a student will find many answers that will not apply to "George Washington."

More important, integrating databases into the social studies curriculum provides the opportunity to incorporate information literacy skills, basic skills essential to 21st-century learners. Students must become competent and independent consumers of information to be productive citizens in the 21st-century workplace. Information literacy skills—the ability to locate, evaluate, and effectively use information—must not be taught in isolation; the skills must be integrated across all contact areas, utilizing the resources of the school library media center. Therefore, collaboration between the social studies teacher and the librarian is essential.

The school librarian, acting as an instructional consultant, can assist the social studies teacher in making critical decisions regarding which information literacy skills are required to meet both the national and state curriculum standards. For every unit in the curriculum, the social studies teacher needs to provide the opportunity to locate, access, comprehend, analyze, synthesize, and create information and knowledge. Students at every level need to be taught the information-processing strategies critical for carrying out these tasks. The school librarian can provide the resources to enable the social studies teacher to integrate these literacy skills into the curriculum.

The chart in Figure I.8, Database Searching and Information Literacy Skills, demonstrates how database searching incorporates information literacy skills to help students become independent lifelong learners.

Some databases are open to all, that is, permit public access; other databases are restricted to certain users and require a password. Still others require a subscription. Because there is a plethora of online databases available to enhance social studies lessons and help students address concepts, ideas, and issues, the social studies teacher and the school library media specialist can use the checklist in Figure I.9, Evaluating an Online Database Service Checklist, to evaluate and compare online database services.

Deciding on a Database for Your School Library

With so many databases from which to choose and limited budgetary dollars, school librarians and classroom teachers have difficult decisions to make. The following annotated list is intended to be an aid in the decision-making process, although the best way to decide to evaluate a database is to try it out with classroom teachers and students. Doing some homework prior to choosing a database will pay off in the long run. Databases offer features that the internet does not. For instance, Google will not translate information from one language

Database Searching and Information Literacy Skills

Information Literacy Skill	Database Searching
Defining/Focusing	Students recognize that an information need exists and make preliminary decisions about the type of information needed based on prior knowledge.
Selecting tools and resources	After students decide what information is needed, they develop search strategies for locating and accessing the appropriate, relevant databases in the school library.
Extracting and recording	Students examine the databases for readability, usefulness, currency, and bias. Some questions they may ask are: Who created the database? What bias might the author have? How current is the information? What expertise might the writer have? Is the database itself a complete list of available data on the topic? Students skim or listen for key words in order to find main ideas/concepts and take notes.
Processing information	After recording information, students examine and evaluate the data in order to use the information retrieved. Students must interact with the information by categorizing, analyzing, evaluating, and comparing for bias, inadequacies, omission, errors, and value judgments. Based on their findings, they either move on to the next step or do additional research.
Organizing information	Students effectively sort, manipulate, and organize the information they retrieved. They make decisions about how to use and communicate their findings.
Presenting finding	Students apply and communicate what they have learned via a research report, project, illustration, dramatization, portfolio, book, book report, map, oral/audio/visual presentation, game, bibliography, etc.
Evaluating efforts	Throughout this process, students evaluate their efforts. They reflect on their efforts to determine the effectiveness of the whole research process. The final product may be assessed by the teacher and the librarian.

Figure I.8: Database Searching and Information Literacy Skills

From *Beyond the Textbook: Using Trade Books and Databases to Teach Our Nation's History, Grades 7–12* by Carianne Bernadowski, Robert Del Greco, and Patricia L. Kolencik. Santa Barbara, CA: Libraries Unlimited. Copyright © 2013.

Evaluating an Online
Database Service Checklist

Criteria	Questions to Ask
Scope/Depth	• How is the database organized? • What is the breadth and depth of the database? How many journals, newspapers, and magazines are regularly indexed? How many scholarly periodical titles are available? • What other features are included in the database? Are there reference books, or other printed reports? Who authors these items? • What is the time span/coverage? How current is the database? • Is the database in English only? Are other languages represented? • Is there an inclusion/index policy? Can teachers/library media specialists suggest materials to be considered for inclusion? • How aligned is the content to the school curriculum? • How integrated is the content with regard to textbooks and state and national standards? • Is the vocabulary suitable for the grade levels?
Ease of Use	• Are there tutorials available for training teachers, library media specialists, and students? • How much extra teaching time needs to be invested in order to teach students the basics of the database? • Is the database search system forgiving? (That is, if a typo is made, are possible search terms suggested? Are there vocabulary lists for searching?) • How well are the screens labeled? Is the layout consistent and user-friendly?

Figure I.9: Evaluating an Online Database Service Checklist

From *Beyond the Textbook: Using Trade Books and Databases to Teach Our Nation's History, Grades 7–12* by Carianne Bernadowski, Robert Del Greco, and Patricia Kolencik. Santa Barbara, CA: Libraries Unlimited. Copyright © 2013.

to another, while a database has that ability. Additionally, many databases offer the option of listening to an audio version of the information, while the internet does not offer that feature in most cases. Most databases will allow you to effortlessly email an article to yourself, while the internet does not offer that feature. Many times, if you want information sent to your email, you have to cut and paste the article or information into a word document, save the document, and then send it in an email message. Furthermore, a database offers age-appropriate articles for the topics your students are researching. When students use the internet, they must often navigate material that is written for adults and not at their appropriate reading level. Finally, databases offer students MLA/APA citations. When students find information that interests them on the internet, they must tackle the laborious job of finding the author of a page, which may be impossible, as well as locating supporting bibliographic information. A database furnishes that information at the bottom of the page in most cases.

The following is an online resource about how to effectively choose a database: <http://www.gplivna.eu/papers/choose_database.htm#_Toc183880189>.

The following is a list of databases, with annotation, that school librarians may find helpful in their own search for appropriate databases for their collections.

INFOBASE LEARNING: FACTS ON FILE

Infobase Learning has a plethora of history databases from which to choose, including those in the following areas:

U.S. History

- African-American History Online
- American Women's History Online
- American Indian History Online
- American History Online
- U.S. Government Online
- Issues and Controversies in American History Online

World History

- Ancient and Medieval History Online
- Modern World History Online
- World Geography and Culture Online
- World News Digest Online

Facts on File by *Infobase Learning* has been published weekly since 1940. It includes curriculum tools for educators such as writing activities, discussion questions, and position papers on a variety of historical and current events. The world history section starts at 1000 BC, so students can find information on all history topics taught in middle and high school history classes. The encyclopedia and almanac include valuable information and maps that students can print or teachers can display on their smart boards. Streaming videos are available on demand for classroom use. Finally, all citations are included for students in both APA and MLA, which makes this extremely user friendly. The one disadvantage of this database is that curriculum tools for teachers are printer friendly but not in a .pdf file, so saving this to one's desktop would be difficult, although librarians and teachers can email it to themselves.

InfoTrac–Cengage Learning

Gale Student Resources in Context by Cengage Learning is an all-inclusive database that encompasses *biographies, government, history, literature, science,* and *social issues.* Students, classroom teachers, and school librarians will find a wealth of information within this particular database. Students can take advantage of the various resources each topic contains, such as audio, references, primary sources, critical essays, academic journals, images, and magazines. The toolbar is helpful for classroom teachers as well as students. Students can access the various maps or images for quick searches, and classroom teachers and school librarians will find the state and national standards alignment extremely helpful in planning for their respective classrooms. Standards can be found for seven different countries, making this database extremely versatile. Teachers will find the standards aligned with what they are currently doing in their classrooms. Students will find "Featured News" on the side of the main page, and they can easily bookmark articles, maps, and so on as they research. Additionally, they can email the information to themselves or a friend. Citations are printed at the end of each resource for easy access by students. The one disadvantage to this database is the simplicity of the maps. Students might find more detailed maps in other resources.

ABC-CLIO Database

ABC-CLIO History and American Government databases offer students an abundance of research and references resources at their fingertips. Students can conduct a search or browse the easy-to-navigate resources established on each site. Students can easily save their searches into an individualized search toolbar or email their resources to themselves or classmates. Classroom teachers and school librarians will find their innovative teaching resources invaluable, and ABC-CLIO has integrated 21st-century challenges for critical thinking into each of its secondary-level databases. Once students learn how to properly navigate one of ABC-CLIO's databases, they then have the skills to easily navigate all databases. Furthermore, databases are updated weekly and help students to easily see the connections between history and current events.

BIBLIOGRAPHY

Beck, Isabel L., et al. *Questioning the Author: An Approach for Enhancing Student Engagement with Text.* Newark, DE: International Reading Association, 1997.

Beck, Isabel L., et al. "Questioning the Author: A Yearlong Classroom Implementation to Engage Students with Text." *Elementary School Journal,* March 1996: 385–414.

Beyer, B. K. *Inquiry in the Social Studies Classroom.* Columbus, OH: Merrill, 1971.

Campbell, J. *The Power of Myth.* New York: Doubleday, 1988.

Gerwin, D., and J. Zevin. *Teaching U.S. History as Mystery.* Portsmouth, NH: Heinemann, 2003.

Hirsh, E. D. "First, Do No Harm." *Education Week,* January 15, 2010: 31.

"Historical Novel." © Encyclopedia Britannica, Inc. May 22, 2011. Available at Dictionary.com <http://dictionary.reference.com/browse/historicalnovel>.

Historical Novel Society. "Defining the Genre." 2011. Available at <http://www.historicalnovelsociety. org/definition.htm>.

Indrisano, R., and J. Paratore. "Using Literature with Readers at Risk." In B. Cullinan (Ed.), *Invitation to Read: More Children's Literature in the Reading Program*, 138–149. Newark, DE: International Reading Association, 1992.

Kuhrt, B., and P. Farris. "Facilitating Learning: Strategic Instruction in Social Studies." In P. Farris and S. Cooper (Eds.), *Elementary Social Studies: A Whole Language Approach*, 131–156. Madison, WI: WCB Brown & Benchmark Publishers, 1994.

Levstik, L., and K. Barton. *Doing History: Investigating with Children in Elementary and Middle Schools* (3rd ed.). Mahwah, NJ: Erlbaum, 2005.

National Council for the Social Studies. Curriculum Standard for Social Studies, 1991. Available at <http://www.ncss.org/standards>.

National Council for the Social Studies. Technology Position Statement and Guidelines, 2006. Available at <http://www.socialstudies.org/positions/technology>.

Palincsar, Annemarie Sullivan, and Ann L. Brown. "Interactive Teaching to Promote Independent Learning from Text." *The Reading Teacher*, April 1986: 771–777.

Phillips, V., and C. Wong. "Tying Together the Common Core of Standards, Instruction, and Assessments." *Phi Delta Kappan*, February 2010: 37–42.

Readence, John, et al. *Content Area Reading: An Integrated Approach*. Dubuque, IA: Kendall Hunt, 1981.

Rosenblatt, L. *Literature as Exploration* (4th ed.). New York: Modern Language Association, 1983.

Savage, T. V., M. K. Savage, and D. G. Armstrong. *Teaching in the Secondary School* (6th ed.). Upper Saddle River, NJ: Pearson Merrill Prentice Hall, 2006.

Schmoker, M. *Focus: Elevating the Essentials to Radically Improve Student Learning*. Alexandria, VA: ASCD, 2011.

Strickland, D. S., and D. E. Alvermann. "Learning and Teaching Literacy in Grades 4–12: Issues and Challenges." In D. S. Strickland and D. E. Alvermann (Eds.), *Bridging the Literacy Achievement Gap, Grades 4–12*, 1–13. New York: Teachers College Press, 2004.

Vacca, R. T., J. L. Vacca, and M. E. Mrza. *Content Area Reading: Literacy and Learning across the Curriculum* (10th ed.). New York: Allyn & Bacon, 2010.

Wineburg, S., and D. Martin. Reading and Rewriting History. *Educational Leadership*, 62(1) (September 2004): 42–45.

1

Native Americans: An Introduction to Teaching This Time Period

NATIVE AMERICANS: RESISTANCE AND ACCOMMODATION

In 1492, when Christopher Columbus sailed from Spain in search of a more direct route to India, he instead landed in the Caribbean and encountered a new world and a new people. Little did he know that his discovery would set in motion a chain of events that would forever change the lives of Native Americans. Columbus was not concerned about the origins or the identities of these people, for he had fully expected to find the land occupied. As Mark Q. Sutton notes in *An Introduction to Native North America*:

> *Europeans wanted to believe that they had "discovered" a new land, untouched and pristine, a land occupied by wandering, primitive savages who did not "properly" possess the land. They believed it their duty to drag the native populations from their state of savagery into the light of civilization. These beliefs served to justify the conquest of the New World and are still widely held today. (2000, 1)*

When studying the evolution of Native Americans and their culture from the 15th to the 20th century, students should be encouraged to define and analyze the causes and effects of the European expansion in North America and the subsequent impact of these actions on Native Americans. Classroom teachers and library media specialists should guide students in investigating the differing cultures, beliefs, and values that led to the conflict, and eventual coexistence, of these vastly different societies.

EXPLORING THE NEW WORLD

The first phase of European activity in the Americas began with the Atlantic Ocean crossings of Christopher Columbus, who was sponsored by Spain. Columbus was followed by other explorers, such as John Cabot, who reached Newfoundland and was sponsored by England. Pedro Cabral reached Brazil and claimed it for Portugal. Amerigo Vespucci, working for Portugal, established that Columbus had reached a new set of continents. *Cartographers* still use a Latinized version of his first name, *America*, to refer to the two continents. Other explorers included Giovanni da Verrazzano, sponsored by France; Samuel de Champlain, who explored Canada; Henry Hudson, who sailed for the Dutch and explored the region

European Explorers and the New World

Date	Explorer	Nationality	Sponsor	Lands Explored
1492	Christopher Columbus	Italian	Spain	Carribean
1497	John Cabot	Italian	England	Newfoundland
1500	Pedro Cabral	Portuguese	Portugal	Brazil
1502	Amerigo Vespucci	Italian	Portugal	Caribbean and South America
1513	Vasco de Balboa	Spanish	Spain	Panama and the Pacific Ocean
1524	Giovanni da Verrazzano	Italian	France	Mid to North Atlantic Coast
1524	Samuel de Champlain	French	France	Canada
1609	Henry Hudson	English	Netherlands	New York area

Figure 1.1: European Explorers and the New World

of present-day New York; and Vasco de Balboa, who crossed the Isthmus of Panama and led the first European expedition to the Pacific Ocean. Eventually, the exploration of these men led to the establishment of colonies up and down the eastern coastline of North America. These key explorers and their nationalities, along with their sponsoring countries and the lands they explored, are noted in Figure 1.1.

Though the reason for the establishment of these colonies varied, ultimately they resulted in a negative effect on the Native American population: "New territory could enhance a nation's power and prestige. Conquered peoples would be converted to Christianity. New land could provide wealth from mining, farming, or trade for governments, investors, and settlers" (Sutton 2008, 24). For example, the Spanish came in search of gold and silver, while the French were primarily interested in fur trading. The English, on the other hand, were interested in religious freedom, while also seeking to increase landholdings in the New World. Not only were the *conquistadors* and other settlers coming with the intention of taking the natural resources from this new land, but "they hoped that the labor would be provided by the native peoples, who could be forced to work for their new masters" (Clark 26).

NATIVE AMERICAN SOCIETIES: CONFLICT AND CHANGE

While European nations were competing for the best trade route to the Far East, Native American societies were experiencing their own periods of change and conflict. According to *Who Built America?*:

Between the twelfth and fifteenth centuries large Native American settlements declined and their populations dispersed to villages. Wars erupted over access to land and resources.

Five groups in the North East (the Mohawk, Oneida, Kayuga, Onondaga, and Seneca) formed the Iroquois Confederacy in the fifteenth century, apparently to reduce such conflict between them. The Confederacy, though, aggravated tensions with other groups. (Clark 13–14)

There were two determining factors that influenced how the Native American societies of North America would interact with Europeans. First, the Native American groups of North America were not organized in the same way as the Native American populations of Central and South America. For example, the Inca and Aztec empires were comprised of major cities with concentrated populations. In contrast, the Native American societies of the North American continent were more scattered, less organized, and in some cases *nomadic*. This difference in organizational structure led to the relatively quick demise of the Aztec and Inca empires, as the Spanish invaders could easily target their prey: "Few North American groups faced such rapid collapse. However, their dispersion and disunity made cohesive response or resistance to invasion difficult to attain" (Clark 13).

The second major factor involved European-imported diseases that infected humans, animals, and plant life. *Epidemics* of smallpox, influenza, typhus, and measles overran the Native American population. The Europeans also introduced new seeds, plants, and domesticated animals to the North American continent and unintentionally brought the diseases of those plants and animals along with them. The Native Americans did not have *immune systems* developed to combat these new and devastating diseases. An example of this would be the fact that "in 1633, a major small pox *epidemic* swept through the region and wiped out entire groups in the first widespread population decline. Many settlers viewed the epidemics among the Indians as an act of God to depopulate the region in order to make room for the colonies" (Sutton 2008, 304).

THE CULTURAL DIVIDE

Also impacting the Native American populations' interaction with Europeans was the diversity of their cultural backgrounds. One aspect of *culture* can be tied to a group's primary mode of subsistence. Harriet J. Kupferer, in her book *Ancient Drums, Other Moccasins*, argues that "culture, in general, is an adaptive system: a collection of strategies and patterns people devise to obtain and use resources in their environments" (4). According to Kupferer, Native Americans can be grouped by four different methods of subsistence: *foragers, part-time gardeners, affluent hunters and fishermen,* and *intensive farmers. Foragers* were Native American groups who were partially nomadic and totally dependent on flora and fauna for their survival; they followed a hunting and gathering tradition for their livelihood. *Part-time gardeners* were populations that combined hunting and gathering with agriculture. Their gardening was not as intensive as that of full-time farmers, and did not involve storage or preservation. *Affluent hunters and fisherman* lived in areas rich in resources, such as forests and along rivers. These areas had sufficient food supplies to allow for cultural development and sophistication. Lastly, *intensive farmers* relied much more heavily on cultivating the land versus hunting and gathering. This form of subsistence allowed for permanent villages and more complex social and political organizations. Obviously, Native Americans demonstrated diversity in their means of subsistence and in general in how they interacted with their environments. Further, their varied means of subsistence led to their being forced to make adjustments and adaptations as European invasions pushed them from one environment to another. For example, malnutrition resulted from forcing hunter-gatherers to become *agriculturists*. In addition, in many cases Native American groups were relocated to areas that they were ill equipped to subsist in, or, in extreme cases, to harsh lands that made survival almost impossible.

Of course, there was a great disconnect between Native American traditions, beliefs, and values and those of European settlers. Among the most basic differences was the value Europeans placed on individual land ownership and wealth versus the Native Americans' desire to live in balance with nature. Europeans believed that through the act of staking out a parcel of land, an individual could claim ownership of that parcel. The concept of individual ownership of an actual piece of ground was foreign to the Native American way of thinking. Indian tribes fought over the use of land. In other words, they fought over hunting, fishing, and/or farming rights to certain pieces of land. But they did not believe that individuals could actually own the land. Because this concept of land ownership was fundamentally incomprehensible to Native Americans, "even after they had made deals with the Europeans for the purchase of land, the meaning of what they had done was often unclear and led to further conflict" (Sage).

Another cultural difference that existed was between the way Native Americans and Europeans viewed warfare. Native Americans viewed the ability to fight hard and endure pain and physical punishment as a sign of honor. In Indian warfare, the victor would claim the women and children of enemy tribes as loot. The Europeans viewed this as primitive and *barbaric*. In turn, European practices, such as hanging, were viewed by Native Americans as destruction of the soul.

As Henry J. Sage has noted, "The arrival of the Europeans also upset the balance of power among the North American Indian tribes, both in the eastern woodland regions and later on the Great Plains and in the deserts of the southwest." For example, in 1641, the Iroquois began a concerted effort to defeat their enemy, the Hurons. For the next 40 years, the Iroquois succeeded in defeating not only the Hurons but many other groups in the central northeast: the Erie, Shawnee, Miami, Illinois, and others. By 1687, remnants of the defeated groups had joined the French and begun to attack the Iroquois. This union resulted in the Iroquois being forced to withdraw from much of the territory that they had conquered (Sutton 2008). Though this infighting among the central northeast Indian tribes greatly distracted the Iroquois nation and weakened their position against the European invaders, they continued to dominate the northeast until the American Revolution.

The role of women in society is another example of cultural differences between Europeans and Native Americans. In eastern tribes, women frequently held power, and in fact, some were tribal chiefs. In Iroquois society, for example, while males appeared to hold political power, in reality, women generally controlled the men. On the other hand, Europeans viewed women as silent and powerless within their culture, their roles largely limited to motherhood and domestic labor. In essence, an *elitist attitude* prevailed, which held that Indians were savages in need of fixing. Native American women were particularly invisible, as European men viewed all women as inferior.

ADAPTATIONS AND ACCOMMODATIONS

Initially, Native Americans tried to *indoctrinate* Europeans settlers into their own systems of authority (Clark). For example, in 1614, Powhattan offered Pocahontas in marriage to John Rolf in an effort to control the English. In another instance, a Wicomesse leader told Maryland's governor in 1633 that "since . . . you are heere strangers and come into our Countrey, you should rather confine yourselves to the Customes of our Countrey, than impose yours upon us" (cited in Clark 52). Clearly, the Native American chieftains in these instances were attempting to communicate with, and manipulate, these European invaders. They were communicating their unhappiness and unwillingness to change, reminding the European visitors that they were guests in the Native American lands and that the Europeans should adapt to the Native American way of life.

Over time, many small skirmishes led to more major battles, and while Indians had small victories, European settlers ultimately gained control of the Americas. More than 400 treaties were signed between the U.S. government and various Indian people: "Many of these agreements were entered into in good faith by respective governments, only to be broken by aggressive white settlers, or less often, by young Indian men continuing to raid after peace had been declared" (Sutton 2008, 29).

Throughout this struggle, Native Americans slowly adapted in order to survive. At first, Native Americans wanted metal products, which they could not make themselves, such as axe heads and knives. Later, they realized the value of guns. Having guns and horses (introduced by the Spanish) completely changed the way Native Americans hunted for food. Native Americans further adapted to the European influx by serving as guides and interpreters, and in many cases fought side –by side with Europeans for common causes.

Tragically, the dramatic decline in the Native American population, in tandem with the fragmentation of Native American groups, tribes, and nations, resulted in the loss of their culture over several hundred years: "As the people who knew the ceremonies, songs, stories, technology, and other traditional knowledge died, less and less of this information was passed along to the next generation. After populations had stabilized and began to rebound, much had already been lost. Territory was also lost, making it even more difficult to reconstitute and rebuild cultures" (Sutton 2008, 38).

The history of the interaction between the Native Americans and the Europeans that began with Columbus is a long and tragic story of greed, with the relentless seizing of more and more land by the Europeans. The Europeans' insatiable thirst for power and wealth led to their eventual domination of Native American civilizations. The effects of cultural differences between Native Americans and Europeans and their American descendants continue to be visible to this day; racism, discrimination, despair, and poor health care are still widespread. Alcoholism is the most serious health problem facing Native Americans today. In some tribes, the rate of alcoholism is as high as 85 percent (Sutton 2008, 38). Yet it is important to realize that despite the death, disease, and destruction brought on by the European invasion, the Native Americans were not transformed into helpless pawns. They are committed to retaining their vibrant cultures and struggle mightily to adapt to ever-changing environments.

Keywords and Terms

1. affluent hunters and fishermen
2. agriculturalists
3. barbaric
4. cartographers
5. confederacy
6. conquistadors
7. culture
8. elitist attitude
9. epidemic

10. fauna

11. flora

12. foragers

13. immune system

14. indoctrinate

15. intensive farmers

16. nomadic

17. part-time gardeners

18. subsistence

BIBLIOGRAPHY

Clark, Christopher, Nancy Hewitt, Joshua Brown, and David Jaffee. *Who Built America?* Boston: Bedford/St. Martin's, 2000.

Kupferer, Harriet J. *Ancient Drums, Other Moccasins.* Englewood Cliffs, NJ: Prentice Hall, 1988.

Sage, Henry J. "Native American Cultures." *Academic American.* 05/15/2010. December 4, 2010. <http://www.academicamerican.com/colonial/topics/nativeam.htm>.

Sutton, Mark Q. *An Introduction to Native North America.* Boston: Allyn & Bacon, 2000.

Sutton, Mark Q. *An Introduction to Native North America.* Boston: Pearson, 2008.

"Ways Europeans Changed Native Americans." *Native American History.* December 4, 2010. <http://www.mce.k12tn.net/indians/blueprint/conflict2.htm>.

2

Native Americans: Book 1

Title: *Indian Captive: The Story of Mary Jemison*
Author: Lois Lenski
Grade/Age: Ages 9–12
ISBN: 9780064461627
NCSS Standards: 1,2,3,4,5,6,8

ANNOTATION

Mary "Molly" Jemison is taken captive by the Seneca Indians and must find her place in her new surroundings. She befriends Little Turtle and comes to understand and accept the ways of her captors. Lenski was awarded a Newbery in 1946 for her historical account of Mary Jemison's life. This timeless classic will captivate readers of all ages.

SUGGESTED VOCABULARY

blood root, bridle, corn pone, embroidery, flax, fodder, frontier, furrow, garrisons, guttural, hemlock, hummocks, musket, perilous, piteous, plundering, puncheon, regalia, sassafras, settlements, skeins, solace, sycamore, thicket, tomahawk, tributaries, wampum, wash basin

BEFORE READING: PREPARING TO JUMP INTO THE BOOK

KWL

Students complete the KWL found in Figure 2.1 in small groups. Students complete the K (What I *Know*) column with information they know about Indian life. Encourage students to write down anything related to Indians, such as settlement locations, dress, customs, and so on. Students then write information in the W (What I *Want* to Know) column before beginning their research. The questions written in this section should guide students' research on the topic. After researching Seneca life in the next activity, students complete the L (What I *Learned*) column. This can serve as a framework for discussion about life as a Seneca.

KWL

What I Want to _Know_	What I _Want_ to Learn	What I _Learned_

Figure 2.1: KWL

Seneca Lifestyle and Traditions

Students visit the website <http://www.native-languages.org/seneca_culture.htm> to investigate the Seneca lifestyle and traditions. Students complete the Seneca Fact Sheet in Figure 2.2 with 20 facts they have learned about the Seneca tribe. Once students compile their list, bring the class together to share all facts with their peers. The classroom teacher or school librarian then writes the facts on chart paper for display in the classroom or library. While reading the novel, ask students to add to the list as they learn more about the Seneca Indians from the text.

Wall Wisher Conversations

Students use <wallwisher.com> to post questions and answers to a prompt provided by the classroom teacher and/or school librarian. Students read primary documents (found in the school library's history database or on the internet) about life as an Indian captive. Then, assign half of the class to act as "captives." The other half of the class asks pertinent and relevant questions of the captives. All students must have a solid foundation of what it means to be an Indian captive in order to participate. Students dialogue on <wallwisher.com> by asking and answering questions.

Conducting a Book Talk

Conduct a read aloud of *A Picture Book of Sacagawea* by David Adler and illustrated by Dan Brown. Be sure to include plenty of prereading, such as predicting, before reading the book. Storybooks have the unique ability to teach history in a user-friendly manner that makes it interesting to children of all ages. Next, require students to find additional picture books about Indian life from either a captive's point of view or a captor's point of view. Students are required to read the picture book and bring it to class to conduct a book talk. Students can use the following guidelines for their book talk:

1. Show the cover of the book or display on the table for the audience to view.
2. Hook your audience with a fact, quote, or interesting detail from the book or from history.
3. Tell your audience the historical context for the book and suggest why the author may have chosen to write about this topic.
4. Describe the book's plot, but do not give away the ending.
5. Tell the audience what can be learned from this book for children, teens, and adults alike.
6. Recommend that others read the book.

DURING READING: GUIDED DISCUSSION QUESTIONS

1. Describe the setting at the beginning of the book.
2. Describe Mary (Molly). How is she similar to you? How is she different?
3. Mary's father says "Injuns." What does he mean? Is the dialect difficult to read? Why or why not?
4. Mary's mother stopped singing in Chapter 1. What does this signify? What might this foreshadow?
5. Why do you think Mary's father is afraid of the Indians? Would you feel the same way? Why or why not?

Seneca Lifestyle and Traditions

Individual Research	Class Findings
1.	
2.	
3.	
4.	
5.	
6.	
7.	
8.	
9.	
10.	
11.	
12.	
13.	
14.	
15.	
16.	
17.	
18.	
19.	
20.	

Figure 2.2: Seneca Fact Sheet

6. Describe the scene when the Indians enter Mary's house. Why do you think there are four Frenchmen there?
7. Describe Mary's family's captivity. How does she react? Do you think you would react the same or differently?
8. Why do you think Mary's father will not eat during the captivity march?
9. Mary is given moccasins to wear. Why?
10. Describe how Mary cares for Davey when the Indians take them from their families.
11. What is the journey like for Mary and Davey once they are taken from their families? Explain. How do they cope with this? How would you react?
12. Mary meets another captive named Nicolas Porter. Describe him. What does Mary hope will happen once she meets him? Does her hope come true?
13. Describe Fort Duquesne.
14. On pages 40–41, Mary is optimistic that help will come for her. Why? What indicates that she may be saved?
15. Why do you think the Indians paint the captives' faces red? What does the red paint signify?
16. What happens when Mary tries to escape?
17. Why is the peach tree at Fort Duquesne so dear to Mary? What does it signify?
18. Mary is given to an Indian woman at the end of Chapter 3. What do you predict will happen to Mary?
19. Describe the two Indian women that take Mary.
20. Why do the Indian women throw away Mary's clothes? Why does she get so upset? Explain.
21. Describe the ceremony in the cabin.
22. Why do the Indian women call Mary "Corn Tassel"? Why is this name ironic?
23. Describe Mary's dream on her first night as an Indian girl.
24. What is the first Indian word Mary learns? Why?
25. Why is Mary forbidden to speak English? How does this make her feel? How would it make you feel?
26. What does Mary do with the corn cake given to her to eat?
27. On page 82, the author writes that "the forest was a cruel enemy." What does this mean?
28. Describe Little Turtle.
29. What does Mary do each day she is sent to fetch water?
30. Little Turtle tries to give Mary a silver brooch. How does she react? Why?
31. Describe Chief Standing Tree. Do you trust him? Why or why not?
32. Mary sees Shagbark again. Who is he? What kind deed does he do for her?
33. Mary learns to speak the Seneca language. Who teaches her? Why is this important?
34. Why is Mary sent to bed without supper?
35. Describe how white and Indian babies are raised differently. In what ways are their upbringings the same?
36. Mary learns many lessons that help her to assimilate into Indian life. Name three things she learns (see page 110).
37. Mary learns that her Indian name has great meaning. What is the meaning? How would her father react to this?
38. Who is Kah Kah?
39. Why do the Indians respect Kah Kah?

40. Mary realizes that she is beginning to think like an Indian woman. Cite an example of this from the text.
41. Predict why Mary and Shining Star are returning to Fort Duquesne. What happens when she returns?
42. Why doesn't Mary stay at Fort Duquesne? What would you have done?
43. On page 141, the author writes, "A second captivity more painful than the first, because her hope was gone." Interpret this line.
44. Describe the Purification Rite Ceremony. What is the significance of the corn husk doll?
45. Describe Earth Woman. What important lessons does she teach Mary?
46. Why does Mary fight the children to not take home the bear cubs as pets?
47. Describe Mary and Little Turtle's relationship.
48. How does Mary react to Little Turtle killing the turkey in the woods?
49. Why does Shagbark change Little Turtle's name? What is his new name?
50. What happens when Mary is reunited with Fallenash?
51. What news does Fallenash share with the Indians?
52. What does Mary ask of Fallenash?
53. Compare and contrast Indian and white men's treatment of women. How are they the same? How are they different?
54. How does Mary react to the newly arrived white captive? How would you react? Did she react the way you expected? Why or why not?
55. Describe the gauntlet.
56. Who is Running Deer?
57. Describe Mary's relationship with Running Deer.
58. Why is Running Dear not permitted to hunt?
59. Describe how the women made sugar.
60. Shagbark gives Running Deer a canoe. Explain what Running Deer does. How does Mary react to this?
61. How is Mary rewarded for making her first cooking pot?
62. Mary shows herself to the English visitors. Explain why this is a mistake.
63. Mary finally learns what happened to her family and their home. How does she react? How do you think you would react?
64. Why is Mary afraid to speak with Captain Morgan?
65. Why does Gray Wolf want to sell Mary to the Englishmen? Why doesn't Mary want to go?
66. Mary finally earns a new Indian name. What is it? What does it mean? Why does she earn a new name?
67. Were you surprised by the ending of the story? Why or why not?

AFTER READING: CONNECTING TO THE TEXT

Letters to Mary: Making the Decision to Stay or Go

Students work with a partner to brainstorm a list of reasons that Mary Jemison should either stay with the Seneca Indians or try to escape. Using the Letters to Mary Brainstorming Sheet in Figure 2.3, students comprise a list of reasons to "stay" and write those reasons in the column. Then, students complete a list of reasons she should "go" and write the reasons in the column. Students should refer to the text for support. Once students have reviewed their lists, they should decide if they believe Mary should have stayed with the Indian tribe or attempted to escape. Students write a letter to Mary convincing her of their opinion. Their letter should include why they think Mary should stay or go and support their decision with explicit examples from the text. Use the Letter Rubric found in Figure 2.4 for assessment purposes.

Visualization Comes to Life: Creating a Class Mural

Students choose an image that represents Indian art from the internet or from a library book or magazine. Using butcher paper, allow students to create a class mural that represents their reactions to and interpretations of the book. Allow students to use paints, pencils, charcoal, or crayons, depending on their preference. Display the mural in the library or hallway for others to appreciate. For students who do not consider themselves artists, invite them to use words instead of images to convey their unique message. All students should be actively involved in the creation of the mural.

Mapping Mary's Travels

Require students to create a map that depicts Mary's travels as an Indian captive. Students should produce both a narrative and a visual of her journeys.

Creating a Podcast

Students create a podcast show about the book. Using both speech and music, students create an entertaining podcast about the book, a character(s), and/or Seneca life. A podcast is *a digital recording of a radio broadcast or similar program, made available on the Internet for downloading to a personal audio player or computer*. Students can create their podcast in an mp3 format or other popular format for class and/or public consumption. Students can upload their creation to garageband.com or iTunes.com. The following websites can assist students in the creation of their work:

<http://www.how-to-podcast-tutorial.com/what-is-a-podcast.htm>
<http://www.podcastingnews.com/articles/How-to-Podcast.html>
<http://radio.about.com/od/podcastin1/a/aa030805a.htm>

Students' podcasts should be accurate; well rehearsed; and free from grammar, spelling, and pronunciation errors. They should also include graphics that enhance the podcast.

The Podcast Rubric found in Figure 2.5 can be used for assessment purposes.

DIGGING INTO THE DATABASE

Reader's Theater

Using the court document of the *Chippewa Indians of Minnesota vs. the United States*, require students to write a script for the court hearing. Students can access the course document from the school library database, or they can find it at <http://openjurist.org/307/us/1/chippewa-indians-of-minnesota-v-united-states>. Students should use the database to investigate additional information about the Chippewa Indians to provide a context and background on the tribe. Once the script is written, students should perform the script in reader's theater format. Costumes are optional and students are permitted to use their scripts. Reader's theater improves fluency and comprehension through repeated readings over an extended period of time. Provide students with plenty of time to practice and prepare the performance for classmates or an audience. You can assess students on the script writing portion of the assignment. Use the Script Writing Rubric in Figure 2.6 for assessment purposes.

Letters to Mary Brainstorming Sheet

Stay	Go

Figure 2.3: Letters to Mary Brainstorming Sheet

Letter Rubric

Evaluation Criteria	3 (Excellent)	2 (Average)	1 (Poor)
Position/Persuasive	The letter's position is extremely persuasive/convincing in nature.	The letter's position is somewhat persuasive/convincing in nature.	The letter's position is not persuasive in nature.
Introduction	The introduction is strong and interesting and brings the reader into the story.	The introduction is somewhat strong and interesting and brings the reader into the story.	The introduction is weak OR no introduction is apparent.
Support	The letter has a clearly stated opinion and contains at least five (5) different and logical reasons for the stated opinion.	The letter has a clearly stated opinion and contains at least four (4) different and logical reasons for the stated opinion.	The letter is either lacking a clearly stated opinion or contains three (3) or fewer reasons for the stated opinion.
Transitions	The writer uses transition words effectively between sentences and paragraphs.	The writer uses transition words between sentences and paragraphs in a somewhat effective manner. Some errors exist.	The writer does not use transition words effectively between sentences and paragraphs OR no transitions are used.
Conclusion	The conclusion of the introduction restates all the reasons in one sentence effectively.	The conclusion of the introduction restates most of the reasons in one sentence.	The conclusion of the introduction does not restate the reasons or is not apparent.
Mechanics	There are 0–1 errors in capitalization, punctuation, and/or grammar.	There are 2–3 errors in capitalization, punctuation, and/or grammar.	There are 4 or more errors in capitalization, punctuation, and/or grammar.

Figure 2.4: Letter Rubric

From *Beyond the Textbook: Using Trade Books and Databases to Teach Our Nation's History, Grades 7–12* by Carianne Bernadowski, Robert Del Greco, and Patricia L. Kolencik. Santa Barbara, CA: Libraries Unlimited. Copyright © 2013

Podcast Rubric

Criteria	Exemplary (5)	Proficient (3)	Incomplete (0)
Introduction	Podcast accurately informs the audience what to expect of the podcast in a clever way and establishes a clear purpose for the podcast. Includes the date, speaker, and setting.	Podcast informs the audience what to expect and establishes a purpose for the podcast. Includes the date, speaker, and setting.	Podcast does not inform the audience what to expect OR does not establish a purpose for the podcast OR does not include the date, speaker, and/or setting.
Content	Accurate information is presented, and follow-up questions are relevant. The content of the interview is highly engaging and interesting to listeners. Open-ended questions are used and relevant.	Accurate information is presented, and follow-up questions are relevant. The content of the interview is somewhat interesting to listeners. Open-ended questions are used but are not particularly relevant.	Inaccurate information is presented, OR follow-up questions are irrelevant. The content of the interview does not engage listeners in any way. No open-ended questions are used.
Delivery of Content	Well-rehearsed delivery of content is apparent. Highly effective enunciation of material. Pacing is exceptional.	Rehearsed delivery, enunciation is effective, and pacing is acceptable.	The content was not rehearsed, and the delivery was weak. The enunciation and pacing of content are distracting to the listener.
Professionalism in Speech	All language is appropriate in grammar usage and professional in nature. No slang terms are used in the podcast.	Most language is appropriate in grammar usage, and some slang terms are used in the podcast.	Poor grammar usage is used throughout the podcast, and many slang terms are used.
Audio/Visual	Graphics are highly relevant to the topic and are copyright free or permission was obtained.	Graphics are relevant to the topic and are copyright free or permission was obtained.	Graphics are irrelevant to the topic OR not copyright free.

Figure 2.5: Podcast Rubric

Script Writing Rubric

	4	3	2	1
Grammar & Spelling	Writer makes 1–2 errors in grammar or spelling.	Writer makes 3–4 errors in grammar or spelling.	Writer makes 5–6 errors in grammar or spelling.	Writer makes more than 6 errors in grammar or spelling.
Capitalization & Punctuation	Writer makes 1–2 errors in capitalization and/or punctuation.	Writer makes 3–4 errors in capitalization and/or punctuation.	Writer makes 5–6 errors in capitalization and/or punctuation.	Writer makes more than 6 errors in capitalization and/or punctuation.
Written in Script Format	The script is written in the correct format. All lines have the correct margin and punctuation.	The script is mostly correct. Either the margin OR punctuation is incorrect.	The script is slightly correct. Both the margins and the punctuation are incorrect.	The script is NOT written in script format.
Creativity	The story contains many creative details and/or descriptions that contribute to the reader's enjoyment. The author has really used his or her imagination.	The story contains a few creative details and/or descriptions that contribute to the reader's enjoyment. The author has used his or her imagination.	The story contains a few creative details and/or descriptions, but they distract from the story. The author has tried to use his or her imagination.	There is little evidence of creativity in the story. The author does not seem to have used much imagination.
Writing Process	Student devotes a lot of time and effort to the writing process (prewriting, drafting, reviewing, and editing).	Student devotes sufficient time and effort to the writing process (prewriting, drafting, reviewing, and editing).	Student devotes some time and effort to the writing process but is not very thorough.	Student devotes little time and effort to the writing process.
Easy to Understand & Follow	Script is easy for a reader to understand and follow. It flows and makes sense.	Script has parts that are confusing but the overall intention is clear.	Script is difficult to read and understand. It does not flow. An attempt has been made.	Script does NOT make sense. Reader can not follow or understand the intention of the script.

Figure 2.6: Script Writing Rubric

From *Beyond the Textbook: Using Trade Books and Databases to Teach Our Nation's History, Grades 7–12* by Carianne Bernadowski, Robert Del Greco, and Patricia L. Kolencik. Santa Barbara, CA: Libraries Unlimited. Copyright © 2013

Photograph Concept Map

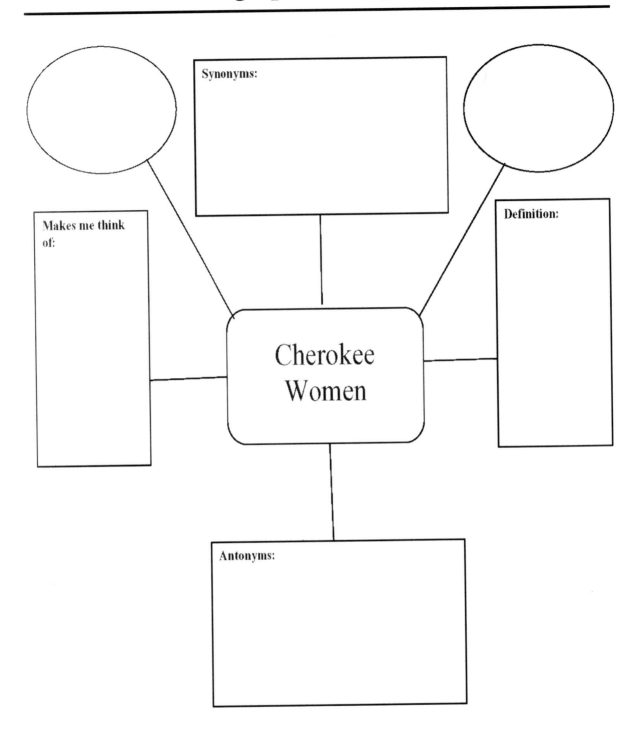

Figure 2.7: Photograph Concept Map

From *Beyond the Textbook: Using Trade Books and Databases to Teach Our Nation's History, Grades 7–12* by Carianne Bernadowski, Robert Del Greco, and Patricia L. Kolencik. Santa Barbara, CA: Libraries Unlimited. Copyright © 2013.

Story Writing Rubric

Criteria	1	2	3	4
Organization	Ideas and scenes are not sequential and/or have no order to their organization. No transitions are used.	This story is a little hard to follow and not always sequential. Some transitions are used.	The story is pretty well organized. One idea or scene is misplaced sequentially. Transitions are used.	The story is very well organized. The story is in sequential order and many transitions are used correctly. Readers are drawn into the story at many levels.
Conflict	No conflict is apparent in the story.	A conflict is present but has no relationship to the plot.	There is a conflict and it has a somewhat clear connection to the plot.	There is a clear, distinct conflict in the story that related directly to the plot.
Resolution	There is no evidence of a resoltuion to the problem.	The resolution is present but has no connection to the conflict and/or plot.	The resolution is somewhat related to the conflict and/or plot.	There is a clear, distinct resolution to the conflict and plot.
Conventions	There are 5 or more mechanical errors.	There are 3–4 mechanical errors.	There are 1–2 mechanical errors.	There are no mechanical errors.
Characters	The main characters are not named and/or described.	The main characters are named but not described.	The main characters are named and described.	The main characters are named and clearly described in text.

Figure 2.8: Story Writing Rubric

From *Beyond the Textbook: Using Trade Books and Databases to Teach Our Nation's History, Grades 7–12* by Carianne Bernadowski, Robert Del Greco, and Patricia L. Kolencik. Santa Barbara, CA: Libraries Unlimited. Copyright © 2013

Venn Diagram

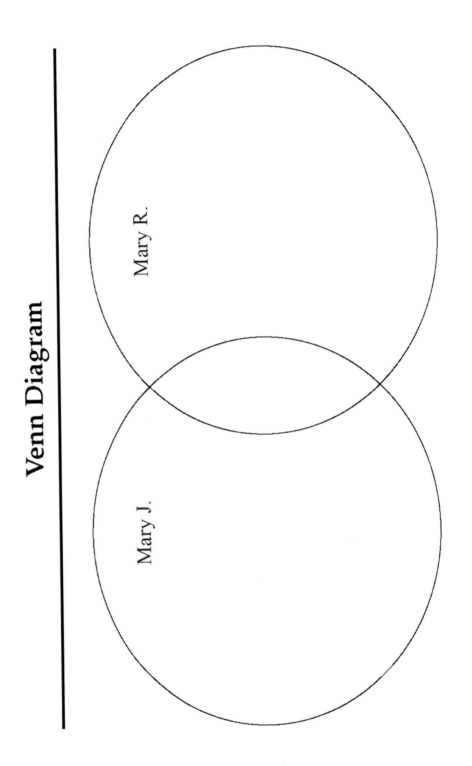

Mary R.

Mary J.

Figure 2.9: Venn Diagram

Cherokee Women: Using a Photograph for Story Writing

Students view an image or photograph of a Cherokee woman. They can find images or photographs from their school library database or on the internet. Students use the Photograph Concept Map in Figure 2.7 to brainstorm ideas, words, or phrases that come to mind while viewing the photograph. Prompt student discussion by asking the following questions:

- What do you think the women were doing right before the photograph was taken? After?
- Tell me their history.
- Where do they live? Work? Play?
- What do she and her family do for fun?

Any questions that will prompt students to think about the photograph in depth will encourage students to think creatively. Next, students are required to write a narrative story about a day in the life of the woman. Encourage students to create a vivid setting; interesting character descriptions; and conflict, resolution, and dialogue between the women. Allow students to be as creative as they wish. Students can work alone or with a partner. Use the Story Writing Rubric in Figure 2.8 for assessment purposes.

Compare and Contrast

Students read the narrative account written by Mary Rowlandson about her time in captivity. The account can be found at <http://www.library.csi.cuny.edu/dept/history/lavender/rowlandson.html> or found in the school library's history database. After reading the narrative, students use the Venn diagram found in Figure 2.9 to compare the story of Mary Rowlandson with the story of Mary Jemison. After completing the Venn diagram individually, the classroom teacher or school librarian should facilitate a discussion with the group.

READ ALIKES

Among the Indians by Herman Lehmann ISBN 9780826314178 (Young Adult/Adult)

Birchbark House by Louise Erdrich ISBN 9780786814541 (Ages 9–12)

The Captured: A True Story of Abduction by Indians on the Texas Frontier by Scott Zesch ISBN 9780312317898 (Young Adult/Adult)

Morning Girl by Michael Dorris ISBN 9780786813582 (Ages 9–12)

Nine Years among the Indians, 1870–1879: The Story of the Captivity and Life of a Texan by Herman Lehmann ISBN 9780826314178 (Young Adult/Adult)

Reservation Blues by Sherman Alexie ISBN 9780802141903 (Young Adult/Adult)

Sign of the Beaver by Elizabeth George Speare ISBN 9780440479000 (Young Adult)

Sing Down the Moon by Scott O'Dell ISBN 9780547406329 (Ages 9–12)

Thunderwoman by Nancy Wood ISBN 9780525454984 (Young Adult)

Where the Broken Heart Still Beats: The Story of Cynthia Ann Parker by Carolyn Myer ISBN 9780152956028 (Ages 9–12)

3

Native Americans: Book 2

Title: *Canyons*
Author: Gary Paulsen
Grade/Age: Young Adult
ISBN: 9780440210238
NCSS Standards: 1,2,3,4,5,6,8

ANNOTATION

Coyote Runs, a young Apache warrior, participates in his first raid and dies tragically. More than a hundred years later, Brennen Cole, a young boy the same age, finds a skull during a camping trip to the canyons near El Paso, Texas. Brennen searches for answers to his questions about the skull with the help of a pathologist, his high school teacher, and, eventually, his mother.

SUGGESTED VOCABULARY

Apache, arroyo, bridle rope, cantina, churning, El Paso, exultation, fissure, forlorn, Fort Bliss, gullies, hostiles, marauding, mesquite, morgue, pathologist, prudent, raids, remorse, vaqueros, warble, warrior, yucca plant

BEFORE READING: PREPARING TO JUMP INTO THE BOOK

Wiki Posting and Discussion

Create a wiki space for your students free of charge at <http://www.wikispaces.com/content/for/teachers>. Require students to use the internet to find five facts about Apache life. To prevent students from doing a general search, assign them a specific topic to research. Topics may include: Apache Warrior, Apache language and culture, Apache weapons, Apache history, Apache mythology, Apache traditions, and/or photographs of Apaches. Students post their information on the wiki and other students comment and begin a discussion of the information. Encourage students to add additional information if they find a discussion warrants that type of engagement. As with all online platforms, use caution and be sure to make the wiki only available to your students for this particular project. The school librarian can help classroom teachers build a safe platform for students.

El Paso PowerPoint

Working in pairs or small groups, students create a PowerPoint presentation to introduce vital facts about El Paso, Texas, the setting of the story. Have each pair or small group research a specific topic so that all areas of interest are covered. Topics should include:

- History of El Paso
- Indian settlements in El Paso
- Apache Tribe
- Caddo Tribe
- Bidai Tribe
- Commerce
- Modern-day El Paso
- Areas of interest

This list is just a beginning. Allow students to create topics and categories as they learn more information during their research. Each group should create at least eight slides for the presentation. Review the PowerPoint Rubric in Figure 3.1 as a guide before beginning the project. The presentation can be assessed using the Presentation Grade Sheet in Figure 3.2.

Making a Dream Catcher

Dream catchers were made for children to catch the nightmares they may have had while sleeping. Use the directions for making a dream catcher at <http://www.ehow.com/how_2044932_make-dream-catcher.html> and teach students how to make their own dream catchers either for themselves or for a younger sibling or relative.

Reading to Children

Introduce students to the world of children's historical fiction by sharing a book about Native Americans written specifically for children, either fiction or non-fiction. Model before reading strategies such as prediction, picture walk, vocabulary discussion, author, and illustrator. As you read the book and show the illustrations, model for students how to confirm or revise predictions and ask questions that help students not only display their comprehension but make connections to the text on many levels. After reading, model for students how to ask questions to provoke comprehension of text and discussion of important details. Then, prepare students to read a book to younger children in an elementary school or library. For planning purposes, ask students to complete the Story Reading Activity in Figure 3.3. This guide will serve as their lesson plan for the reading. They should include all questions they will ask, as well as page numbers where they will stop for predictions and questions. Encourage students to use sticky notes for stopping points during the story.

The following is a list of books from which to choose:

- *Ten Little Rabbits* by Virginia Grossman
- *Fire Race: A Karuk Coyote Tale of How Fire Came to the People* by Jonathan London
- *The Girl Who Loved Wild Horses* by Paul Goble
- *Death of the Iron Horse* by Paul Goble

PowerPoint Rubric

Criteria	Exemplary (3)	Proficient (2)	Partially Proficient (1)	Incomplete/ Unsatisfactory (0)
Slides	Contains 8 or more slides	Contains 6–7 slides	Contains 4–5 slides	Contains 3 or less slides
Text	Text is easy to read with font sizes that vary appropriately. Excellent usage of text and font size.	Fonts are generally easy to read and font sizes vary.	Overall readability of text is somewhat poor. The presentation includes too much text and/or too many varying font sizes.	Overall readability of text is very poor due to font sizes that are too small to read and/or too much text. This is inappropriate for the assignment.
Graphics	All graphics are highly related to the content and highly appropriate in size and quality. Images are professional in quality and nature.	Most graphics are related to the content and appropriate in size and quality. Images are professional in quality and nature.	Some of the graphics are unrelated to content and/ or distract from the presentation OR graphics are poor in quality and/or nature.	Most graphics are unrelated to content and district from the presentation. Graphics are poor in quality and nature.
Mechanics	No errors in grammar, capitalization, punctuation, or spelling.	1–2 errors in grammar, capitalization, punctuation, or spelling.	3–4 errors in grammar, capitalization, punctuation, or spelling.	5 or more errors in grammar, capitalization, punctuation, or spelling.
Content	Content is highly relevant and related to the topic. It is research based and topic is covered in depth.	Content is relevant and related to topic. Topic is covered.	Content is somewhat related to the topic but lacks depth or much research.	Content is not related to the topic and lacks the necessary research.

Figure 3.1: PowerPoint Rubric

Presentation Grade Sheet

Name _____

Presentation of concept—23 points

Explained the concept thoroughly	5	4	3	2	1	0
Included research	5	4	3	2	1	0
Engaged audience	5	4	3	2	1	0
Spoke professionally			3	2	1	0
Dressed professionally	5					0

Total points _____ /23

Comments:

Figure 3.2: Presentation Grade Sheet

Story Reading Activity

Using the children's book of your choice, plan a read aloud including before, during, and after reading activities. Complete the guide below.

Before
During
After

Figure 3.3: Story Reading Activity

- *The Rough-Face Girl* by Rafe Marti
- *The Legend of the Bluebonnet* by Tomie dePaola
- *The Legend of the Indian Paintbrush* by Tomie dePaola
- *Coyote: A Trickster Tale from the American Southwest* by Gerald McDermott
- *Grandmother's Pigeon* by Louise Erdrich

DURING READING: GUIDED DISCUSSION QUESTIONS

1. The first sentence of the book is, "Soon he would be a man." What does that make you think of? What do you predict will happen? To whom is the author referring?
2. You meet Coyote Runs in Chapter 1. How old is he? What makes this summer different than previous summers for this young man?
3. What is the name of Coyote Runs's tribe? Why does he want to become a "man"?
4. Describe how Coyote Runs views his mother. How does he treat her? Explain.
5. Describe Sancta. Who is he? What is his role in the Apache Tribe?
6. Going on a raid makes Coyote Runs a man. Why do you think this is true?
7. Describe Brennen Cole. Describe his relationship with his mother.
8. On page 12, Brennen meets Bill Halverson. Brennen says that the meeting changed his life. Predict what might happen.
9. What do you think is Coyote Runs's purpose for going to Mexico? Why?
10. Describe the raid.
11. Why do you think the Apache tribe is fighting with the Mexicans?
12. On page 62, Coyote Runs thinks a bullet cannot penetrate his medicine. What do you think this means? Explain.
13. How does Coyote Run end up riding on his horse next to the Mexican warrior? What do you think will happen next?
14. Describe Magpie. Do you think you would like to be his friend? Why or why not?
15. Explain why you think a horse meant wealth for members of the Apache tribe.
16. Compare and contrast Bluebellies and Mexicans.
17. Coyote Runs feels "stupid" after the raid. Explain why you think he feels this way.
18. Describe what happens to Magpie on page 71. How does Coyote Runs react? How would you react? What happens to Coyote Runs?
19. Describe what happens when Coyote Runs hides in the canyon. Would you have done the same? Explain.
20. Brennen awakes, in the present day, at his campsite in the canyons. What wakens him? What does he find beneath his sleeping bag? If you were Brennen, would you call the police? Why or why not?
21. Describe Brennen's dream the night he returns home from the canyons. What do you think the dream means? What might his dreams foreshadow?
22. At the end of Chapter 12, Brennen's dreams force him to find answers. What do you predict he will do to find those answers?
23. From whom does Brennen seek help? Why? Where do they go? Would you have asked for help with the mystery of the skull? Why or why not?
24. What do Brennen and Homesley learn about the skull from the pathologist at the morgue?
25. Describe the morgue scene.
26. What is a Murphy Drip?

27. What happens when Brennen's mother finds the skull? Do you think she over-reacts?
28. Brennen secretly wishes Homesley were his father. Why do you think this is true? Do you think Homesley would make a good father? Why or why not?
29. Describe what Brennen learns when he finds the patrol orders. How does he feel?
30. Brennen realizes he must return the skull. Where is he taking it? Why must he take the skull to that location?
31. Describe what happens at the canyons when Brennen returns? How does his mother help him?
32. On page 180, Brennen thinks, "And it is so that I would have been free, been safe, if I had beaten them to the medicine steps. . . ." What does this mean?
33. Describe how the conflict is solved and the story comes to a logical resolution. Were you satisfied with the ending? How might you have changed the story if you were the author?
34. Create a new title for the book.

AFTER READING: CONNECTING TO THE TEXT

Point of View Audio Journals

Typically, journal entries are written in a notebook or diary. Challenge students in small groups to write a journal entry from either Brennen's point of view or Coyote Runs's point of view and record that entry in audio format. Allow students to work in pairs or small groups to write the entry (script) and then use the available technology to record the entry. An alternative is to allow students to create a PowerPoint presentation and include the journal entry as a voice over. Audio recordings can be created in an mp3 format and uploaded to <garageband.com>, while PowerPoint presentations can be uploaded to <teachertube.com> or <schooltube.com>. Students can use the Collaboration Checklist in Figure 3.4 to self-assess their work.

Making a Movie Trailer

Students create a movie trailer for the book as if it has been turned into a movie. Allow students to view several book trailers on teachertube.com or schooltube.com so they can understand what is expected of them. Remind students that movie trailers are meant to entice viewers to go to the movie theater but do not give away the ending. Students create a rough draft or concept draft on paper as they brainstorm ideas in small groups or pairs. Students sketch each image and text with special notes they can use when creating their trailer. Students can find storyboard templates online or simply take a plain piece of white paper and fold it into sections, with each section representing a scene for the movie trailer. Once students have completed their rough drafts and the classroom teacher or school librarian has approved them, they can create the trailers using Photo Story3 software from Microsoft, Windows Media Player, iMovie, or similar software available from the school's technology department. Once they have completed their movie trailers, students can upload their videos to the school website or to a video sharing site. Students can use images, narration, and music. The following websites will help students find images:

- Wikimedia: <http://wikimedia.org/>
- Galileo: <http://www.galileo.usg.edu/>

Collaboration Checklist

Group Member: _____

Name of Project: _____

Answer each question honestly as you evaluate your own contributions to the group project. Support your rating with an example.

Task	Strong	Okay	Weak	Example
I contributed fully and equally to this project.				
I worked more than the other members of the group.				
I contributed ideas.				
I helped write the assignment.				
I helped revise and edit the assignment when appropriate.				
I helped in the production of the project.				
I performed tasks that were not asked of me.				
I met with members of my group outside of class or library time.				

Figure 3.4: Collaboration Checklist

- Library of Congress American Memory Project: <http://memory.loc.gov/ammem/index.html>
- Library of Congress Prints & Photographs Reading Room: <http://www.loc.gov/rr/print/catalog.html>
- Clipart.com: <http://www.clipart.com/en/>

Use the Book Trailer Rubric found in Figure 3.5 for assessment purposes.

Pantomime

Students choose their favorite scene, and without words, act out the scene. The remainder of the class tries to guess what part or scene of the book is being portrayed.

Writing a Summary Using Signal Words

Students write a succinct summary of a chapter using signal words discussed in the introduction (*first, second, before, during, then, finally, for example, for instance , different, as opposed to, instead of, although*). Students share their summaries in the order in which the chapters "are presented in the book. Students can vote on what they feel is the best summary using the most effective transition words.

DIGGING INTO THE DATABASE

Creating a Tri-Fold Brochure

Using the school library's database as a resource, students create a tri-fold brochure about the Apache Indian tribe, Apache culture, Apache warriors, or other topic that would highlight Apache life in some way. Students can create their brochure using Microsoft Word or publishing software. Images from the database can also be added. The brochure should be informative, include a variety of information, and be inviting to readers. Classroom teachers and school librarian can use the Tri-fold Brochure Rubric in Figure 3.6 for assessment purposes.

Teacher for the Day

Students use school library's database to create a history lesson to teach their peers. Students can choose any topic as long as it is related to the book in some way. Topics for students to consider might include:

- Apache life
- Apache Indian Tribe
- Apache culture
- Apache warriors
- Geronimo
- Treaty of Medicine Lodge
- Carlos Montezuma
- Kiowa
- Native American treaties

Movie Trailer Rubric

Qualifiers	Exemplary (4)	Proficient (3)	Partially Proficient (2)	Incomplete (1)
Content	Themes are presented in a highly logical order and related to the book. The movie trailer does not give away the ending of the book. The trailer really piques the viewer's interest.	Themes presented in a somewhat logical order, and the trailer does not give away ending of the book. A viewer would most likely be interested.	Themes are related to the book but not in a logical order, and/or the trailer does not give away the ending of the book.	Themes are not expressed and the ideas are not in a logical order. The trailer gives away the ending of the book.
Images, Graphics, and Sounds	All of the images, graphics, and sounds enhance the content of the movie trailer. All images, graphics, and sounds are of high quality.	Most of the images, graphics, and sounds contribute to the understanding of content of the movie trailer. Most of the images and sounds are high quality.	A few of the images, graphics, and sounds are inappropriate for the content of the movie trailer and/or some of the images and sounds are not high quality.	Images and sounds are inappropriate and do not create interest or understanding of the movie trailer, and the quality of sound and images are poor.
Layout	Fonts chosen are appropriate in size and easy to read and follow. The format is consistent throughout the presentation.	Fonts chosen are appropriate in size and easy to follow. The format is usually consistent throughout the presentation.	Fonts chosen are somewhat difficult to read and vary throughout the presentation. Some of the format is inconsistent throughout the presentation.	Fonts chosen are difficult to read and follow throughout the presentation. The entire format is inconsistent.

Total:_____

Figure 3.5: Movie Trailer Rubric

From *Beyond the Textbook: Using Trade Books and Databases to Teach Our Nation's History, Grades 7–12* by Carianne Bernadowski, Robert Del Greco, and Patricia L. Kolencik. Santa Barbara, CA: Libraries Unlimited. Copyright © 2013.

Tri-Fold Brochure Rubric

Criteria	3	2	1
Organization	Each section of the brochure is highly organized.	Most sections of the brochure are organized.	Few sections of the brochures are organized.
Content	All content is accurate.	Most content is accurate.	Little content is accurate.
Content	There are no errors in mechanics.	There are 1–2 errors in mechanics.	There are 3 or more errors in mechanics.
Layout	The layout is highly inviting to the reader. There is not too much on one page or section and enough white space is provided.	The layout is somewhat inviting to the reader. There is too much or too little white space on some of the pages.	The layout is not inviting to the reader. The information is crammed onto the page or there is too much white space provided. It is very difficult to read.
Layout	The graphics are highly appropriate and complement the material being presented.	The graphics are somewhat appropriate for the material being presented.	The graphics are inappropriate for the material being presented.
Total			

Figure 3.6: Tri-Fold Brochure Rubric

From *Beyond the Textbook: Using Trade Books and Databases to Teach Our Nation's History, Grades 7–12* by Carianne Bernadowski, Robert Del Greco, and Patricia L. Kolencik. Santa Barbara, CA: Libraries Unlimited. Copyright © 2013

Round Table Discussion Sheet

Topic: _____

Source: _____

Summary of discussion:

Discussion points:

*

*

*

*

*

*

*

*

*

*

*

Figure 3.7: Round Table Discussion Sheet

Students write a lesson plan detailing how they will present the information in an engaging and interactive manner. Allow students to integrate technology, cooperative learning, or other instructional strategies to make the lesson fun for their peers.

Round Table Discussion

Students use the American government database to find recent information about Native Americans. Divide the class into pairs to research a topic of interest that has a modern-day twist. Students should document their research on the Round Table Discussion Sheet in Figure 3.7 to serve as talking points for their round table. Next, assemble students in a circle in the classroom or library and give each pair of students an allotted time limit in which to present their findings and take questions from the group. Encourage discussion and ask students to reflect on what they have learned from the discussion.

Creating Charts and Graphs

Students choose three Indian tribes and create two different charts to display population in the years 1980, 1990, and 2000. Students can create a pie chart, line graph, bar graph, or related visual. Students can create the charts and/or graphs using online tools or tools found in word processing programs. Students then present their work to the class.

READ ALIKES

Bead on an Anthill: A Lakota Childhood by Delphine Red Shirt ISBN 9780803289765 (Young Adult)

The Birchbark House by Louise Erdrich ISBN 9780756911867 (Ages 9–12)

Children of the Longhouse by Joseph Bruchac ISBN 9780140385045 (Ages 9–12)

Circle of Wonder: A Native American Christmas Story by N. Scott Momaday ISBN 9780826321497 (Ages 9–12)

Cloudwalker: Contemporary Native American Stories by Joel Monture ISBN 9780804111676 (Young Adult)

The Girl Who Helped Thunder and Other Native American Folktales (Folktales of the World) by James Bruchac, Joseph Bruchac, Ph.D., and Stefano Vitale ISBN 9781402732638 (Ages 9–12)

Morning Girl by Michael Dorris ISBN 9780786813582 (Ages 9–12)

Rising Voices: Writings of Young Native Americans by Arlene Hirschfelder (Compiler) and Beverly Singer ISBN 9780804111676 (Young Adult)

The River People by Kristen James ISBN 9780980235005 (Young Adult)

They Called It Prairie Light: The Story of Chilocco Indian School by K. Tsianina Lomawaima ISBN 9780803279575 (Young Adult)

4

Spanish and French Explorers/Settlers: An Introduction to Teaching This Time Period

The study of the Spanish and French exploration of the New World should compare and contrast the motivating factors that drove this exploration and exploitation of North America. For example, though both Spain and France, and the explorers they hired, were driven to find the Northwest Passage to China, the Spanish were focused on the quest for gold and silver and the acquisition of land for the purpose of establishing plantations to grow sugarcane, tobacco, and other crops needed in Europe, whereas the French were primarily interested in settling just enough people to manage the fishing and fur trade conducted at various trading posts. The French were interested in the commercial value that could be realized by tapping the natural resources of this land. They had little interest in settling the land.

THE SPANISH

Spain's New World empire grew out of its conquests at home. On and off, dating back to the 12th century, Spanish rulers and nobles had attempted to drive out or convert Islamic settlers in the south of Spain. The Spanish renewed their conquest around 1450 and finally succeeded in defeating the kingdom of Granada in 1492, thereby expelling or converting its Muslim and Jewish population. From 1470 to 1496, Spanish troops also fought to create a colony on the Canary Islands, eventually wiping out the island's native population. As noted in William Polk's *The Birth of America*, these conquests set patterns that Spain would replicate in the Americas. Buoyed by these conquests, King Ferdinand and Queen Isabella of Castile gave permission for Columbus's voyage just after the fall of Granada. The aim of this voyage was to extend westward the *militancy* that Spain had successfully employed at home (Polk 22).

Columbus was inspired by Marco Polo's travels to the Far East and became obsessed with reaching Cathay (China) by traveling west on the southern Atlantic. With the blessings and finances of King Ferdinand and Queen Isabella, Columbus set sail with a very small *flotilla* of three ships, the Niña, the Pinta, and the Santa Maria. He left Spain on August 3, 1492, and a week later landed in the Canary Islands. On September 6, he set off again, sailing for approximately a month until, on October 12, his crew caught sight of an island in the Bahamas. This island is present day San Salvador (Polk 27–28).

After this initial landing and the exploration of several of the islands, Columbus returned to Spain ("European Exploration"). Leaving the crew of the Santa Maria, which had been wrecked, to build a fort in present-day Haiti, he sailed home, bringing with him a small amount of gold, some coconuts, and a few Native Americans, whom he called Indians (Reich).

On his second voyage, Columbus anchored at St. Croix on November 14, 1493, and took on water at Salt River Bay. While there, several Caribbean natives began firing arrows at the returning boat and several people on each side were killed. Columbus named the area Cabo de las Flechas, or Cape of Arrows. This site marks Columbus's only attempted landing in what eventually became U.S. territory.

Columbus may have been perplexed by the disparity between the islands he had visited and the glowing accounts of Marco Polo, but if he was he did not share his doubts with the Spanish rulers. On the contrary, his report to Ferdinand and Isabella promised that on future voyages he would "procure as much gold as they, the king and queen, needed, as well as spices, cotton, and drugs" (Reich 9). This report so impressed the Spanish *monarchy* that before the end of 1493, Columbus led a *fleet* of 17 ships back to the West Indies.

On this voyage he reinforced the origininal settlement of Haiti and explored Puerto Rico, Jamaica, and the Lesser Antilles. He returned to Spain in 1496, bringing with him 500 Native Americans (of whom 200 died). On his third and final voyage (1502–1504), he sailed along the coast of Central America, insisting that the riches of Asia could not be far away. Two years later he died, poor, bitter, and definitely out of favor with the Spanish court.

Columbus's voyage spurred Spanish and Portuguese exploration and its associated mission of Christian conversion. A legal battle ensued, as each country laid claim to the New World. Eventually, a *compromise* was *mediated* by Pope Alexander VI. This compromise, known as the Treaty of Tordesillas, "drew an imaginary line from the Arctic pole to the Antarctic pole, one hundred *leagues* west of the Cape Verde islands, which were located west of the African coastline. The decision gave Spain the rights to anything west of the line and the opportunity to explore and settle the known new world" ("Spanish and French Exploration," AP Study Notes, <apstudynotes.org>, 2008). Pope Alexander, himself a Spaniard, favored Spain in his decision. This act of arrogance would soon go against Spain when Brazil was discovered east of the treaty line, in Portuguese territory. In 1500, Portugal laid claim to Brazil and over the next century prepared to extend its Atlantic island plantation system to South America.

Within a mere 10 years of Columbus's maiden voyage to the New World, thousands of Spanish *conquistadors*, explorers, and potential homesteaders risked their lives by crossing the Atlantic, seeking the fabled riches of the New World. In particular, their conquests covered the southern portion of the current United States, as well as Mexico, and stretched into present-day South America, specifically the region that is now Peru. Meanwhile, Spain also extended its exploration of the Caribbean. In 1502, Spanish families had settled on Hispaniola and soon were colonizing Cuba, Puerto Rico, Jamaica, and other islands. After 1508, the Spanish made several ventures on to the Central American mainland, and in 1513, Vasco Nunez de Balboa confirmed that the Americas were a separate continent when he crossed the Isthmus of Panama and became the first European to see the Pacific Ocean.

Driven by their voracious hunger for gold, the Spanish felt justified in the *heinous* acts they performed against the Native Americans. The military prowess of the Spanish conquistadors, in tandem with the institution of slavery and the introduction of European diseases, together broke the spirit of the Native American population. Native American weaponry was no match for the "modern" weaponry of the conquistadors. Likewise, the conquistadors' employment of horses, which Native Americans had never seen before, provided them with a decided advantage in squelching any resistance by the natives. There was no greater example of the Spanish *annihilation* of Native Americans than the defeat of the Aztecs. In the Aztec capital of Tenochtitlan, the emperor learned of this Spanish activity as early as 1508, but he punished priests who foretold of an invasion of what is now Mexico. A decade later, however, conquistador Herman Cortes and his troops marched on the city and captured it. Slaughtering and looting by the Spaniards provoked a revolt and Cortes and his men were driven back. However, three years later, in 1521, Cortes and his men recaptured Tenochtitlan. The capital's fall marked the end of the Aztec empire itself, as fire and disease further contributed to the demise of the Aztec population: "The conquerors soon established Spanish rule and slowly *eradicated* the learning and knowledge base of the Aztec people, as the Spaniards considered them to be a *heathen* civilization" (Clark 24).

While the conquistadors fought in the name of the Spanish throne and for the promotion of Christianity, they were also envious of the Portuguese and their access to African gold. Rumors abounded of fabulous wealth in the Americas. "Those lands do not produce bread or wine," claimed one Spanish writer, "but they do produce large quantities of gold, in which lordship exists" (Clark 24). The Spanish first looted and shipped to Spain the treasures of the Aztec and Inca temples and palaces, but they soon exhausted those riches and began to search for new sources.

The Spanish explorer Juan Ponce de Leon is credited with being the first European to reach that part of North America that would eventually become the United States. Ponce de Leon had a thirst for adventure. He satisfied this thirst by serving on Columbus's second expedition to the New World. No stranger to combat, Ponce de Leon was a member of the nobility and became a soldier in the battle against the Moors. Years later, his military background would provide him with the wherewithal to suppress Indian uprisings on the island of Hispaniola, which today is home to the countries of Haiti and the Dominican Republic. For his efforts, the Spanish throne rewarded Ponce de Leon by bestowing upon him the governorship of present-day Puerto Rico. In 1513, having amassed a fortune in gold and slaves, Ponce de Leon left the governorship of Puerto Rico and devoted his efforts to exploration (Reich 28). He sailed northward in search of two primary treasures—gold and the fabled Fountain of Youth. Ponce de Leon landed in present-day Florida. He and his men dug for gold and bathed in many of the natural springs, but found nothing of any consequence. Though his expedition found little support from the Spanish crown, he was still knighted and granted his second governorship, this time of present-day Florida. It took him until 1521 to *muster* support for a second expedition with colonization as his primary goal. It was during this attempt to colonize Florida that Ponce de Leon was killed, falling victim to an assault by Native Americans. His death marked a period of general disinterest in the region that is now Florida. This lasted several decades, until the French tried to settle in Florida. This French activity drove the Spanish to establish a fort at St. Augustine in 1565. St. Augustine eventually became the first town in the present-day United States. Yet few Spaniards ever settled in Florida, and it remained an isolated *outpost* during the colonial period. The Spanish later settled the land using the mission concept, wherein missions were established and used to bring the native population under control ("European Exploration").

Meanwhile, in another corner of North America Francisco Vasquez de Coronado continued Spain's exploration and *exploitation* of the New World. In 1540, Coronado explored the region stretching from New Mexico as far north as present-day Kansas and the Arkansas River. He led a large expedition of several hundred Spaniards, African slaves, and approximately one thousand Native Americans who were supportive, or at least non-combative, of the Spanish cause. Though Coronado and his company came up empty handed in their quest for gold, silver, and other treasures, they caught first sight of the Grand Canyon in present-day Arizona, and in New Mexico they saw the Zuni's *adobe pueblos*. Coronado was ultimately regarded as a failure, though his travels provided the Spanish with a better understanding of the geography of the American southwest and an introduction to the Pueblo people.

As Coronado continued his journey across the southwest region of North America, a fellow Spaniard, Hernando de Soto, brought Spain back to present-day Florida for further exploration of the southeasternmost region of the current United States. De Soto led one of the best-equipped expeditions of his time, with over 600 armored soldiers and approximately 300 horses. De Soto traveled through Florida and the area that is now North and South Carolina, eventually heading west toward the Mississippi River. He is believed to be the first European to view the Mississippi. Again, with the focus on gold, silver, and other treasure, de Soto's soldiers, fueled by their disappointment, typically attacked the Native Americans and burned their villages.

Hence, Spanish exploration opened the New World to European settlers, and though Spain grew disinterested in North America, Spanish soldiers and priests eventually established approximately 40 mission stations throughout the southeast, predominantly in Florida: "Spanish culture, law, religion, and language gradually blended with those of the Native Americans and African slaves. Thus, Spain had most of the New World to itself during the 16th century, before other Europeans began to take interest" ("Spanish and French Exploration," AP Study Notes, <apstudynotes.org>, 2008). As the French, the English, and the Dutch began to make serious attempts to establish their own American colonies, Spain pushed into present-day New Mexico, building more forts and missions and founding the town of Santa Fe in 1608.

THE FRENCH

As Jerome Reich notes in *Colonial America*, "Spain and Portugal may have thought that they had divided the New World between them, but England and France strongly dissented" (11). In 1497, King Henry VII commissioned a voyage by John Cabot, who was actually of Italian origin (Giovanni Caboto). A Genoese sea captain, Cabot, like Columbus, believed that a route to Asia was waiting to be found by heading westward. Cabot was unable to gain the necessary financial backing from either Spain or Portugal, but he did finally convince England's monarch that his plan was worth funding. His first attempt, in 1495, was unsuccessful; however his second attempt, in 1497, resulted in a successful landfall on the shore of what is today Newfoundland. This discovery gave England its claim to North America: "However, political, religious, and economic turmoil forced England to wait more than half a century before seriously endeavoring to challenge Spain and Portugal" (Reich 11).

Meanwhile, France also had aspirations of tapping the potential riches of the New World, and in 1524, Giovanni da Verrazzano, another Italian navigator, was commissioned by the French crown to sail west in search of new land. In 1524, Verrazzano sailed along the North American coast from the Carolinas to present-day Maine. He was followed by Jacques Cartier a decade later, who sailed into the St. Lawrence River. Cartier followed his initial trip with two more expeditions, sailing up the St. Lawrence as far as Montreal. Efforts to establish a settlement at Quebec were unsuccessful, however. Though the French sought gold and silver, much like the Spanish, once they realized that precious metals were not to be found, they refocused their efforts on fur trapping and fishing in the Canadian north.

By the early 1600s, Samuel de Champlain had established fur trading posts at Port Royal, present-day Annapolis, in Acadia, now Nova Scotia, and at Quebec. The French traded European goods predominantly for beaver skins, which were in high demand throughout Europe, as the European beaver had become extinct. The Hurons, a relatively peaceful people, were among the key Native American tribes trading with Champlain and his people. Though the Hurons were Iroquois, they were not a part of the Iroquois *Confederacy*. As such, Champlain "felt it wise to aid them in their battles against the Mohawks and other Iroquois tribes" (Reich 41). Over time, these battles revolutionized the Native American warfare in eastern North America, as spears, clubs, and bows and arrows were gradually replaced by firearms. And this in turn had an impact on colonial history. Eventually, Champlain's consistent support of the Hurons pushed the Iroquois to *forge alliances* with both the Dutch and the English. This became a critical alliance in later years when the English fought the French for control of the fur trade and associated territories.

Champlain's effort to convince the government to send settlers to Canada were in vain, and in 1627, an English expedition took over Port Royal (present-day Annapolis), followed by a second takeover of Quebec in 1629. These conquests by the English may have aborted the French empire in America and prevented the later struggle between England and France for control of North America. However, a peace treaty soon returned these settlements to France (Reich 41).

By 1633, Champlain returned to Quebec with a group of settlers sent by the Company of New France, which had been granted a monopoly of the fur trade with Canada. Complicating matters for the French, however, was the fact that in the short time that the French and the English were settling their differences, the Iroquois had badly defeated the Hurons, who had become the *middlemen* of the fur trade between the Native Americans of the north and west and the French at Quebec. As stated earlier, the Iroquois had developed an alliance with the Dutch and the English, hence their preference for trading with the Dutch at present-day Albany, rather than with the French at Quebec. Dutch goods were also less expensive than French goods, which added to the Iroquois' *predisposition* to minimize their interaction with the French. This resulted in low profits for the French. Even the French settlement at Quebec 10 years later failed to improve trade with the Iroquois.

By the late 1660s, with encouragement by the French chief minister Jean-Baptiste Colbert, under Louis XIV, the French colonial policy was changed and Canada was removed from the control of the Company of New France and was made a royal colony. The French government exercised minimal rule on its American "empire." *Duties*, or taxes, were simply levied on the import of liquor and tobacco, and *conversely*, on the export of beaver and moose pelts.

Moreover, the French left the governing of New France to three main colonial officials: the governor, the *intendant*, and the bishop. The governor handled military operations and relations with the Native American population, while the intendant was responsible for judicial matters and commercial affairs, as well as local administrative issues. The bishop, of course, was in charge of religious affairs. Even so, with this "local" governing structure in place, the colonization of New France progressed very slowly.

Colbert attempted to promote the settlement of New France by sending hundreds of young men and women to Canada, encouraging them to marry and establish roots in this new land. In spite of these efforts, by 1680, the population of New France was only about 8,000–10,000, with the land being cultivated about a mile inland on either side of the St. Lawrence River. This was because the fur trade still remained the focus of the Canadian economy, and this is what drove the French migration west and south. French fur traders eventually set up trading posts near the Great Lakes where furs could be "purchased" more cheaply. The well-known explorations of the Mississippi River by Father Jacques Marquette and Louis Joliette in 1673, and Robert Cavelier de La Salle, who journeyed to the mouth of the Mississippi in 1682, were both tied to fur trading. Still, the motivation to find the Northwest Passage to China was always present, and though this prize was never found, La Salle's exploration led to France's claim of the Mississippi River Valley.

Working in *tandem* with the enterprising Canadian fur traders were the Jesuits. This Catholic order was interested in converting the Native American population to Catholicism. As did the Spanish priests through their mission system, the Jesuits ministered to the needs of the French settlers while continuing their efforts to convert the Native Americans.

The 17th century saw the establishment of New France, yet the French did not displace the Native Americans as the Spanish had done and as the English eventually were to do. As William Polk noted in *The Birth of America*,

> *The French were never driven by the hunger for land that permeated "British America." Their major thrust was toward trade and trade meant fur. Since they could not catch fur-bearing animals themselves, the French had no incentive to plunder the Indians as the Spaniards did in the Caribbean and in Florida. Rather, they distributed what to them were cheap trade goods in exchange for fur. This exchange gave rise to a new kind of Frenchman, the* coureurs de bois. *(63)*

These young adventurous fur traders, the coureurs de bois (or runners of the wood), not only traded with the Native Americans, but also dressed in their native dress, lived in their native houses, spoke the Native American dialect, and often intermarried with the Native American women. As Polk stated, "More than any other group, they would be the *interface* of Europeans and Native Americans" (63).

During the first half of the 18th century, French posts were established at Detroit, Niagara, Kaskaskia, and Cahokia in the Illinois country and at New Orleans at the mouth of the Mississippi River. These posts put France in control of the entire area from the Allegheny Mountains to the Mississippi River, from Canada all the way to New Orleans.

Keywords and Terms

1. adobe
2. alliance
3. annihilation
4. compromise
5. confederacy
6. conquistadors
7. conversely
8. *coureurs de bois*
9. duties
10. eradicated
11. exploitation
12. fleet
13. flotilla

14. forge
15. heathen
16. heinous
17. intendant
18. interface
19. leagues
20. mediated
21. middleman
22. militancy
23. monarchy
24. muster
25. outpost
26. predisposition
27. pueblos
28. tandem

BIBLIOGRAPHY

Clark, Christopher, Nancy Hewitt, Joshua Brown, and David Jaffee. *Who Built America?* Boston: Bedford/ St. Martin's, 2000.

"European Exploration of the Southeast and Caribbean." Southeast Archeological Center, 1996. December 29, 2011. <www.nps.gov/seac/outline/07-exploration/index.htm>.

Polk, William R. *The Birth of America.* New York: HarperCollins, 2006.

Reich, Jerome R. *Colonial America.* Upper Saddle River, NJ: Prentice Hall, 2001.

5

Spanish and French Explorers/Settlers: Book 1

Title: *Night Journeys*
Author: Avi
Grade/Age: Ages 9–12
ISBN: 9780380732425
NCSS Standards: 1,2,3,4,5,6,8

ANNOTATION

Peter is adopted by a Quaker family eight years before the Revolutionary War. Peter has to decide if catching two runaway indentured servants is worth his own freedom. This coming-of-age novel sheds light on the tough decisions made by young teens in the late 18th century and decisions teenagers still struggle with today.

SUGGESTED VOCABULARY

accoutrement, alacrity, alarum, askance, bondsman, britches, civility, condemnation, constable, contradict, eddies, fathom, felon, hastened, mockery, monotonous, perplexity, petulance, piety, precariously, presumption, prudent, Quakers, rebuke, redemption, retorted, scamps, tumult, unfurling, vexation

BEFORE READING: PREPARING TO JUMP INTO THE BOOK

Quaker Testimonies

Require students to Think, Pair, Share by first asking them to write down everything they know or have heard about Quakers. Then, ask students to read the Quaker Testimonies found at <http://www.quno.org/newyork/Resources/AllQuakerTestimonies.pdf>. Encourage students to take notes as they read, either on the document or on a separate sheet of paper. After students have read the material, ask them to share what they have leaned. It is imperative that students understand the way in which Quakers lived in order to comprehend the novel.

Writing in the First Person

Peter York, the main character in the novel, is taken in by Mr. Shinn, a Quaker minister and Justice of the Peace, after his family dies from an undisclosed disease. Knowing only that, students write a two-page narrative from Peter's point of view from that point forward in the book. Keep in mind that students are not permitted to read Chapter 1 or "peek" at the book. They are predicting what will happen. After students have written their first-person narratives, allow them to share with the class. Have students vote on which of the narratives they think accurately portrays what will happen in the text. After they read the novel, allow students to revisit their predictions and narratives to revise or confirm their initial predictions.

Author Scavenger Hunt

Students work alone or in small groups to answer the following questions about the author, Avi. The author's website is the only source they may use to find information. The website is <http://avi-writer.com/>.

Students answer the following questions:

1. Name five books that Avi has written.
2. Name three reasons Avi writes for kids and not adults.
3. How long does it usually take Avi to write a book? Why do you think this is true?
4. Name Avi's six secrets to good writing. With which do you most agree? Disagree?
5. Name one of Avi's books that was published in 1981.
6. Summarize Avi's newest book, titled *City of Orphans*.
7. Name four awards that Avi has won.
8. Name two of his picture books.

Defining Freedom

Before reading the text, it is important for students to examine their definitions of freedom. Distribute the Concept Map found in Figure 5.1 to students. Ask students to work with a partner to complete the map. After students complete the map, the classroom teacher or school librarian should encourage a class discussion where students work together to create a class definition of the term.

DURING READING: GUIDED DISCUSSION QUESTIONS

1. Describe what happens to Peter's family, as described in Chapter 1.
2. Describe Peter. What qualities to do you admire about him?
3. Describe Everette Shinn's personality. What is your first impression of him? Do you think he will be kind to Peter? What do you know about Peter and Mr. Shinn's relationship so far?
4. At the beginning of Chapter 3, Peter and Mr. Shinn have a disagreement about what issue? Do you think Peter should argue with the man who took him in and gave him food and shelter?
5. Where does Peter go at the end of Chapter 3? Do you think he is too young? Why or why not?
6. Describe the journey of Peter, Mr. Shinn, and the other men.
7. Interpret this quote from page 23: "'The law's a chain that keeps all as one,' he said. 'But mind, it's still a chain.'"

Concept Map

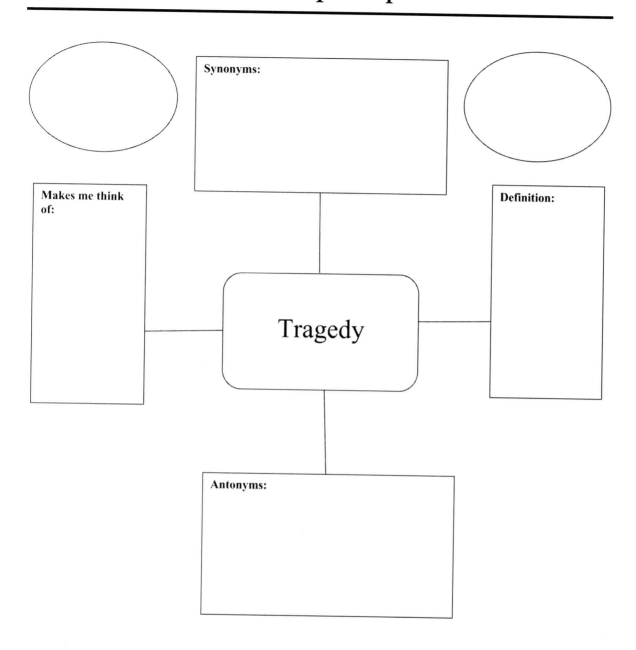

Synonyms:

Makes me think of:

Tragedy

Definition:

Antonyms:

Figure 5.1: Concept map

8. On page 23, Peter describes Mr. Shinn as a hypocrite. What does that term mean? Do you agree or disagree? Support your answers with examples from the book.

9. At the end of Chapter 7, Peter sees someone across the river when he is sitting atop the large rock. Who is it? He then hears gunfire. Who do you expect to be shooting? Why?

10. On page 33, Peter is forced to go back to the island. Why? How does he feel about this? Describe what happens on his return from the island.

11. On page 52, Peter ends up on the Jersey side of the river. Why does he not want anyone to know this has occurred?

12. Describe who Peter meets in the woods. Why does this surprise him?

13. Describe Betsy.

14. Why do Peter and Betsy plan to cross the river?

15. Describe their journey to Morgan's Rock.

16. Peter finally catches his felon at the beginning of Part 3. Describe the scene on pages 71–74. How would you react?

17. On page 91, Peter states, "in time, even that little match for my exhaustion and I slipped into trouble, restless sleep." Explain what this means.

18. Peter decides to free the boy and girl. Explain his decision. Would you make the same choice? Why or why not?

19. Why does Peter decide to flee to Easton?

20. Peter struggles with deciding to do what is morally right and what is legally right. Describe his dilemma. What would you do? Why?

21. What does Mr. Shinn eventually do for Peter and the runaways? Why do you think he is so kind? Does this change your opinion about Mr. Shinn? Why?

22. Peter returns to Mr. Shinn. Why do you think he does this? Would you do the same? Why or why not?

23. Peter is extremely brave throughout the novel. Cite three acts of bravery by Peter.

24. Explain the significance of the title of the book. If you could give the book another title, what would it be?

AFTER READING: CONNECTING TO THE TEXT

Problem Solution: Dealing with the Text

The character in the book faces many problems. Using Figure I.4, Problem and Solution Graphic Organizer (found in the Introduction to this book), require students to identify one major problem in the story and four possible solutions to the problem. Next, require students to sit in a circle and read each of their problems to the class. The class then discusses the "real" solution of the character. The student then reads the possible solutions that could have been implemented by the character. Students should not reveal their characters but require the class to guess each character.

Prezi Presentation

Students work together or with a partner to create a Prezi presentation to share with classmates and for publication on the school library website. Students can pick one of the following topics: Quakers, Revolutionary War, orphans of the Revolutionary War, English colonies, indentured servants, or another topic that is related to the book. Prezi presentations are an alternative to PowerPoint presentations. The presentation should be informative and creative, and captivate the audience. Use the Prezi Rubric found in Figure 5.2 for assessment purposes.

Prezi Rubric

Criteria	3	2	1
Content	All content is accurate and in the student's own words.	Most of the content is accurate and in the student's own words.	Little of the content is accurate and not in the student's own words.
Elements	Includes at least five sections with four or more facts in each. All pathways were easy to follow and sections were grouped logically.	Includes at least five sections with one or two facts in each, OR some pathways were easy to follow and sections were grouped somewhat logically.	Does not include five sections and pathways were neither easy to follow nor grouped logically.
Grammar/Punctuation/Spelling	There are no grammar, punctuation, or spelling errors in the epilogue.	There is one grammar, punctuation, and/or spelling error in the epilogue.	There are two or more grammar, punctuation, and/or spelling errors in the epilogue.

Figure 5.2: Prezi Rubric

From *Beyond the Textbook: Using Trade Books and Databases to Teach Our Nation's History, Grades 7–12* by Carianne Bernadowski, Robert Del Greco, and Patricia L. Kolencik. Santa Barbara, CA: Libraries Unlimited. Copyright © 2013

Sketching a Character

Students work in pairs to create a list of qualities of a character and then challenge their partners to sketch that character from their descriptions. Character descriptions can come directly from the text or from students' interpretations of the text. Students can include physical attributes of the chosen character as well as personality traits. Encourage students to challenge their partners by saving the most obvious clues for last. Distribute the Character Attribute Chart in Figure 5.3 for students to record their character traits; the Sketching a Character Template in Figure 5.4 can be used by the student who is illustrating. Once students sketch a character, it is then their turn to describe a character for their assigned partner.

Checking the Facts

Because the book is classified as historical fiction, there are a wealth of historical facts that can be checked for accuracy. Require students to find 10 facts from the text (location of events, names, dates, etc.) and write the facts in column one of the Checking the Facts Organizer found in Figure 5.5. Next, students use various sources, print and electronic, to check the facts to ensure accuracy. Finally, students share their fact organizer with a peer, who in turn verifies their facts with a second source. To encourage engagement, allow students to switch papers after checking only one fact so that the entire class has a chance to interact with each classmate.

DIGGING INTO THE DATABASE

Writing a News Article

Using the school library's history database, students research the life and politics of the Quakers. Students should use both text and images to research information about the group. Students then write news stories about the Quakers from any angle they desire. The classroom teacher can use the News Article Rubric in Figure 5.6 for assessment of the assignment.

Anticipation Guide for Research

The classroom teacher or school librarian should distribute the Indentured Servant Anticipation Guide found in Figure 5.7. Students answer "yes" or "no" to the questions listed on the anticipation guide. Next, the students are directed to the school library's history database to research indentured servants. By searching and exploring the database, students must find the answers to the questions. Once students have found their answers, they answer "yes" or "no" to the same statements. Bring the class together to compare answers, engage in class discussion, and share additional information learned while researching.

Children of the American Revolution

Students visit the school library's history database and search for two articles about children during the American Revolution. Students then summarize the information learned about the children of the American Revolution. Then, students work with a partner to draw what a child of the American Revolution looked like. Students are encouraged to use the database for images that might aid them in this assignment. Allow students to display their creations in the school library or classroom bulletin board.

Character Attribute Chart

Character's Name: _____

Physical Attributes	Personality Attributes

Figure 5.3: Character Attribute Chart

Sketching a Character Template

Figure 5.4: Sketching a Character Template

Checking the Facts Organizer

Fact	Location	Verified by

Figure 5.5: Checking the Facts Organizer

News Article Rubric

	4	3	2	1
Lead	The article has a strong lead that includes the 5 Ws and is written in an extremely effective manner.	The article includes a lead that includes the 5 Ws.	The article includes a lead but does not include all the required elements.	The article does not include a lead.
Supporting Details	Provides a sufficient number of supporting details that relate directly to the lead.	Provides a number of supporting details that relate to the lead.	Provides one or two supporting details that relate to the lead.	Does not provide any supporting details.
Mechanics	The writing has no mechanical errors.	The writing has 1–2 mechanical errors.	The writing has 3–4 mechanical errors.	The writing has 5 or more mechanical errors.
Spelling	The writing has no spelling errors.	The writing has 1 spelling error.	The writing has 2 spelling errors.	The writing has 3 or more spelling errors.

Figure 5.6: News Article Rubric

From *Beyond the Textbook: Using Trade Books and Databases to Teach Our Nation's History, Grades 7–12* by Carianne Bernadowski, Robert Del Greco, and Patricia L. Kolencik. Santa Barbara, CA: Libraries Unlimited. Copyright © 2013.

Indentured Servant Anticipation Guide

Yes	No		Yes	No
		Indentured servants were often treated as harshly as slaves.		
		Indentured servants had to pay for their passage to America by working as servants.		
		Many indentured servants died due to harsh conditions in America.		
		Indentured servants were permitted to own land, unlike African slaves.		
		"Beating bread" was a common task of indentured servants and considered a desirable job.		

Figure 5.7: Indentured Servant Anticipation Guide

From *Beyond the Textbook: Using Trade Books and Databases to Teach Our Nation's History, Grades 7–12* by Carianne Bernadowski, Robert Del Greco, and Patricia L. Kolencik. Santa Barbara, CA: Libraries Unlimited. Copyright © 2013

Creating a Timeline

Using the school library's history database, require students to work in small groups to create a timeline of the Revolutionary War. Students can make the timeline either by hand or electronically to enhance their knowledge of what happened before (the setting of the book), during, and after the war. This knowledge will enhance their comprehension of the book and add to their existing and expanding historical knowledge base.

READ ALIKES

April Morning by Howard Fast ISBN 9780812415100 (Ages 9–12)

Bloody Country by James Lincoln Collier and Christopher Collier ISBN 9780685100905 (Ages 9–12)

Burr by Gore Vidal ISBN 9780375708732 (Young Adult/Adult)

Drums by James Boyd ISBN 9780689801761 (Young Adult/Adult)

The Fighting Ground by Avi ISBN 9780756984618 (Ages 9–12)

Freelon Starbird by Richard E. Snow ISBN 9780395242759 (Young Adult/Adult)

Hessian by Howard Fast ISBN 9781563246012 (Young Adult/Adult)

I'm Deborah Sampson: A Soldier of the American Revolution by Patricia Clapp ISBN 9780688417994 (Ages 9–12)

Johnny Tremain by Esther Forbes ISBN 9780440442509 (Ages 9–12)

My Brother Sam Is Dead by James Lincoln Collier and Christopher Collier ISBN 9780439783606 (Ages 9–12)

6

Spanish and French Explorers/Settlers: Book 2

Title: *The King's Fifth*
Author: Scott O'Dell
Grade/Age: Ages 12 and up
ISBN: 9780618747832
NCSS Standards: 1,2,3,4,5,6,8

ANNOTATION

Esteban de Sandoval, a mapmaker, is to stand before the royal Audiencia to decide his fate for hoarding gold that he did not share with the king. The year is 1541 and the place is the Fortress of Juan de Ulua, near Vera Cruz, New Spain (Mexico). Esteban records his adventures in the Land of Cibola on paper his jailer, who wants the hidden treasure, has supplied. We learn of Esteban's adventures as he tells his story in retrospect.

SUGGESTED VOCABULARY

cartographer, Cibola, clemency, cudgel, desolate, dialect, doublet, ducats, galleon, islet, labyrinth, maravedis, mica, minotaur, mirage, mutiny, New World, nocturnal, obsidian, stern, tiller

BEFORE READING: PREPARING TO JUMP INTO THE BOOK

Reading Response Log

Introduce students to the concept of using a Reading Response Log while they read. Classroom teachers or school librarians can use the Reading Response Log found in Figure 6.1 as a template for students. This template can be distributed to students at the beginning of each chapter or assigned reading. The classroom teacher or school librarian should model how he or she responds to reading before assigning this task to students. Once students are proficient at responding to the required reading, the instructor might consider allowing students to respond without the template.

Reading Response Log

Part I: Retell what this chapter was about in your own words.

Part II: Respond to the chapter by answering the following questions:

1) This connects to my life in this way . . .

2) I wonder . . .

3) This is important because . . .

4) I don't understand . . . because . . .

5) I would like to learn more about . . . because . . .

Figure 6.1: Reading Response Log

Vocabulary Exploration

Students are given the list of vocabulary terms and asked to define the terms using a dictionary. Then students are required to ask a friend how they would define each term. Next, as students read, they should look for words in the text and complete the "in text" column by defining the word by using the context clues. Finally, students are required to use the word in a sentence. Use the Vocabulary Exploration handout found in Figure 6.2.

Predicting and Confirming Activity (PACA)

Distribute the Predicting and Confirming Activity handout (PACA) in Figure 6.3 before reading the text. Explain to students that proficient and skilled readers naturally predict as they read. As it is important to predict as one reads, it is just as important to revise and/or confirm those predictions. Instruct students before reading a chapter that they should find a classmate and complete the PACA handout and write three predictions for that particular chapter. At the end of each chapter, the classroom teacher and/or school librarian should review the PACA handout.

Watching a Cartoon in Preparation for Reading

Show students an episode of the cartoon *The Mysterious Cities of Gold* and inform students that Scott O'Dell's book inspired this cartoon. Ask students to jot down notes of things that are unclear in the cartoon that may need clarification. They can use that list of questions as a guide while reading to look for answers.

DURING READING: GUIDED DISCUSSION QUESTIONS

1. In the opening pages, describe the setting of the story.
2. Describe the narrator. What is his age?
3. What is the significance of the title of the book? What is the king's fifth?
4. On page 7, the narrator is in a boat. Where is he going and with whom is he traveling?
5. Who makes up Coronado's Army?
6. Describe Mendoza. What are your initial thoughts of him?
7. At the end of Chapter 1, the narrator must make a map of the unknown. What advice does he receive? What would you do?
8. What is Mendoza searching for in Chapter 1?
9. In Chapter 2, why does the narrator feel pressured to volunteer to go look for the man ashore?
10. How are the men outwitted by Alarcon in Chapter 3?
11. Why do the men begin to see mirages?
12. On page 31, the narrator says, "The sun was a leech that sucked the moisture from our flesh." Explain this statement.
13. On page 35, the men find fresh water. Where are the men?
14. At the end of Chapter 6, the men finally meet up with Torres. Why do Torres and Mendoza argue? Why does Mendoza want the narrator to be quiet? How does this make you feel?
15. Why does Zia steal the cartographer's paints?
16. At the beginning of Chapter 8, we find the crew at camp. Where are they going?
17. What is Corte's Law?
18. What is the significance of the name Valley of Hearts?

Vocabulary Exploration

Vocabulary Word	Your Definition	Friend's Definition	In Text	Your Sentence
Cartographer				
Clemency				
Cibola				
Cudgel				
Dialect				
Doublet				
Ducats				
Galleon				
Labyrinth				
Maravedis				
Mica				
Minotaur				
Mutiny				
New World				
Nocturnal				
Obsidian				

Figure 6.2: Vocabulary Exploration

Predicting and Confirming Activity (PACA)

Directions: Before reading each chapter, you and a partner create at least three predictions about the chapter. As you read, confirm or revise your predictions. If your predictions were correct, place a check in the "correct" column, noting the supportive material from the text with page number

*Cross out any incorrect predictions and rewrite them to be correct. Also include support from the text for your corrected prediction.

Chapter Number	Correct?	Prediction	Support (include page number from text)

Figure 6.3: Predicting and Confirming Activity (PACA)

19. In Chapter 9, the old Indian man talks of Hawikuh. What does he tell the men?
20. When we learn that the narrator is telling his story from jail, how do you react? What does he tell his jailor about the treasure? What would you have done?
21. Describe Don Felipo's motives.
22. Where do the men travel after the Red House?
23. In Chapter 10, we learn the narrator's name. What is it? Describe his fight with the Indian. Was he scared? Would you react the same way as Sandoval?
24. Sandoval says, "I am no Spaniard." What does he mean?
25. At the beginning of Chapter 13, the crew comes across the Scarlett Cliffs. What does this mean for them? What do they find?
26. Where does the crew find the gold?
27. Describe how the gold is both a blessing and a curse to the Spaniards.
28. Sandoval hides a gold nugget from the others. Why is this a risk? Would you have done the same? Why or why not?
29. How does Mendoza get the wool he needs to mine the gold? Why is this a mistake?
30. On page 142, Mendoza starts a fire. How does Father Francisco respond to the fire? Why?
31. Of what two crimes is Sandoval being accused?
32. Describe the bartering between Mendoza and the Indian chief on page 179.
33. We learn that the Indians do not value gold. Why do you think this is true?
34. Why do you think trading a horse for gold is against the king's law?
35. Zia rides Blue Star for the first time. What significance does this hold? Explain.
36. Esteban learns that Zia will testify at his trial. How does he react? What happens when he finally sees her? Describe her testimony.
37. Describe what Zia does each time a deer is killed. Why do you think she does this?
38. What is Mendoza's plan for the gold?
39. How does Mendoza really die? Why is Esteban being blamed?
40. Describe the Inferno.
41. In the end, who ends up with the gold?
42. How would you change the ending if you were the author?

AFTER READING: CONNECTING TO THE TEXT

Becoming a Cartographer

Students examine a variety of maps, taking special note of the key. Students then create a map of a fictional place of their own. They are required to draw the map by hand on 11 x 17 paper. Students should include mountains, rivers and other physical features that are necessary map elements and supply a key.

Readers' Theater Script

In small groups, students pick the chapter of their choice and turn the chapter into a readers' theater script. Require students to include a narrator, main characters, and secondary characters. It is most helpful if students chose a chapter that lends itself to multiple speaking parts. The script should be written so that anyone could perform the scene. Require students to create props for their scripts and then perform them for their classmates or young children in the school or library. Classroom teachers or school librarians can use the Readers' Theater Rubric in Figure 6.4 for assessment of the written script.

Readers' Theater Rubric

Category	4	3	2	1
Written Script	The written script is extremely accurate and reflects the original chapter.	The written script is accurate and reflects the original chapter.	The written script is somewhat accurate or somewhat reflects the original chapter.	The written script is not accurate and does not reflect the original chapter.
Written Script	The written script follows the requirements of script writing and includes all stage directions.	The written script follows most of the requirements of script writing and includes all stage directions.	The written script either does not follow the requirements of script writing or does not include all stage directions.	The written script does not follow the requirements of script writing and does not include stage directions.
Delivery of Script	Student read the script with confidence and expression, made gestures, and maintained excellent eye contact.	Student read the script with some expression, gestures, and eye contact.	Student read the script but had little expression, few gestures, or little eye contact.	Student had difficulty reading the script and did not use expression, gestures, or eye contact.
Props	Student used props in a highly effective manner while reading the script.	Student used props in an effective manner while reading the script.	Student did not use props in an effective manner while reading the script.	Student did not use props.

Figure 6.4: Readers' Theater Rubric

From *Beyond the Textbook: Using Trade Books and Databases to Teach Our Nation's History, Grades 7–12* by Carianne Bernadowski, Robert Del Greco, and Patricia L. Kolencik. Santa Barbara, CA: Libraries Unlimited. Copyright © 2013

Question Answer Relationships

Students use the Question Answer Relationship in Figure 6.5 to ask and answer questions related to the text. The classroom teacher or school librarian distributes the discussion questions above to pair of students. Students then read the questions to their partners, and the partners decide if the question is an "in the text" or " in my head" question. The students categorize the questions. Once a question is answered, the students write it on their form. The students then switch roles until their questions are answered and documented on the handout.

Creating a Commercial

Students work in small groups to create a 30-second commercial for the book *The King's Fifth* by Scott O'Dell. Students brainstorm ideas for their commercials and create storyboards before going to production to create their commercial. Students then create a video or audio commercial for the book. The objective is to sell Scott O'Dell's book. Classroom teachers or school librarians can use the Commercial Rubric in Figure 6.6.

DIGGING INTO THE DATABASE

Gold Rush

Esteban is imprisoned because he does not share his gold wealth with the king. Students read *The Bad Luck and Good Luck of James Frazier Reed* by James D. Houston, found at <http://museumca.org/goldrush/ar03.html>.

Then, students search the school library's history database for an additional article about the Gold Rush using the research as an aid. Next, students write a letter to Esteban from a Native American about the impact his gold search had on the Native American's tribe.

Sketching History

Students view several sketches from the school library's history database and then create their own interpretations of the treatment of Native Americans by the Spaniards. Students can create their illustrations with a variety of tools, including paper and pencil, clay, or technology.

Native American Collage

Students research a Native American tribe of their choice using the school library's database. Students should research the customs and history of that tribe. Students then create a collage of the tribe. Students can use photographs from the internet, magazines, newspapers, or other resources they find helpful. Classroom teachers or school librarians can use the Collage Rubric found at <http://www.readwritethink.org/files/resources/lesson_images/lesson1012/VisualCollageRubric.pdf>.

Native American Dress and Customs

Each small group of students uses the school library's history database to research a Native American tribe of their choice. With this research, students will recreate one representation of the tribe's dress and customs. Students can represent this in any way they want.

Question Answer Relationship

In the Text Questions	In My Head Questions
Right There	Author and You
Think and Search	On My Own

Figure 6.5: Question Answer Relationship

Commercial Rubric

Content	3	2	1
Writing	The commercial is well written, portrays the message in an effective manner, and is highly engaging for viewers.	The commercial adequately portrays the message and is somewhat engaging for viewers.	The commercial does not portray the message and is not engaging for viewers.
Benefits	The commercial clearly explains to viewers the benefits of purchasing the book.	The commercial adequately explains to viewers the benefits of purchasing the book.	The commercial does not explain to viewers the benefits of purchasing the book.
Enunciation/ Diction	Presenters' enunciation/diction is excellent.	Presenters' enunciation/ diction is average.	Presenters' enunciation/ diction is below average.
Time Frame	The commercial is 30 seconds in length.	The commercial is between 20 and 29 seconds in length.	The commercial is less than 19 seconds in length.

Figure 6.6: Commercial Rubric

READ ALIKES

At the Moon's Inn by Andrew Lytle ISBN 9780817355494 (Young Adult/Adult)

De Soto and the Conquistadors by Theodore Maynard ISBN 9780404042790 (Young Adult/Adult)

Exploration and Conquest: The Americas after Columbus: 1500–1620 (The American Story) by Betsy Maestro ISBN 9780688154745 (Ages 9–12)

Exploration and Discovery: Everyday Life by Walter Hazen ISBN 9781596470101 (Ages 9–12)

Francisco Coronado by Don Nardo ISBN 9780531165768 (Ages 9–12)

Hernando de Soto: Spanish Conquistador in the Americas by Jeff C. Young ISBN 9781598451047 (Ages 9–12)

Indio by Sherry Garland ISBN 9780152000219 (Young Adult/Adult)

The Latest Word from 1540: People, Places, and Portrayals of the Coronado Expedition by Richard Flint and Shirley Cushing Flint ISBN 9780826350602 (Young Adult/Adult)

No Settlement, No Conquest: A History of the Coronado Entrada by Richard Flint ISBN 9780826343628 (Young Adult/Adult)

The Spanish Frontier in North America: The Brief Edition by David J. Weber ISBN 9780300140682 (Young Adult/Adult)

7

English and Dutch Colonists: An Introduction to Teaching This Time Period

Warfare in much of Europe kept the French, Dutch, and English from focusing much attention on the New World well into the late 1500s. However, in 1604, with the signing of the Treaty of London, the French, Dutch, and English were able to channel their efforts to establish colonies in North America. The English made their first attempt at colonization at Jamestown, Virginia, in 1607, a tiny, *precarious* settlement that barely survived its first year of existence. The French followed in 1608, founding Quebec, and the Dutch followed suit with the establishment of Fort Orange (present-day Albany) on the Hudson River in 1614.

Though France, England, and the Netherlands *vied* with one another to establish a foothold in North America, their colonization efforts, and the motivating factors influencing those efforts, differed greatly. In *Who Built America?* Clark and Hewitt noted,

> *France set out to* dominate *a vast sweep of territory from the St. Lawrence River Valley to the Great Lakes region and down the Mississippi River. The French state backed merchants and* missionaries *who* penetrated *the back country, establishing close relationships with Native Americans and* converting *many to Catholicism. Dutch interest however, was spurred by* commercial ventures *organized by the Dutch West India Company, and focused on the Mid-Atlantic region, especially the Hudson River Valley. Dutch merchants and settlers stayed closer to the coast. They brought their reformed (Protestant) churches with them, but their religious beliefs had less impact on Indian life than those of the French.* (34–35)

Though both the French and the Dutch attempted to establish farming settlements, both countries' major interests lay in the commercial value of the New World, primarily through fishing and the fur trade. Relatively small numbers of French and Dutch citizens were enticed to actually migrate to North America, so colonization progressed slowly. The English, however, took a much more aggressive approach, and, though the English were very much involved in fishing and the fur trade, for many the *quest* for religious freedom drove them from their homeland to the eastern shores of North America to start a new life.

THE DUTCH

Following the English attempt to establish Jamestown colony in 1607 and the French founding of Quebec in 1608 came the Dutch, who were still obsessed with the idea that there was a better way to reach India and the Far East. There were many who believed that by sailing north, above Norway, a shorter, more direct course to the Far East would be found. Therefore the Dutch East India Company *commissioned* Henry Hudson, an English sea captain, to search for the *elusive* passage. Hudson was hired in 1609 and set sail in early April for the Arctic Ocean, as his plan was to sail north of Norway and of Russia, eventually reaching Asia. However, by mid-May Hudson and his crew were forced to turn back as ice blocked their route.

It was at this point that Hudson, as a result of fellow mariners' tales of a western route to the Pacific, elected to change course and sail across the North Atlantic. His intent was to search for the Northwest Passage. It was believed that the Northwest Passage cut across North America and would ultimately lead to the Far East. On July 2, Hudson and his men reached what is now the Grand Banks, south of Newfoundland, followed by a stop on the shores of present-day Nova Scotia. By early August the sailors found themselves near Cape Cod. Hudson, at this point, captained his ship up the mouth of a large river. He and his men sailed as far inland as present-day Albany before changing course and returning to Europe. The large river that they followed inland would eventually bear Hudson's name. Upon his return to Europe, Hudson claimed the entire Hudson River Valley for the Dutch East India Company, even though Giovanni da Verrazano, sailing under the French flag, had visited the area some 80 years earlier. Though the Northwest Passage was never found, the area turned out to be one of the best fur trading regions in North America. The Dutch actually laid claim to the area, based on Hudson's voyage along the Atlantic coast from Virginia to Canada.

Dutch merchants, highly aware of the potential profits to be made in fur trade alone, formed the New Netherland Company in 1614: "By 1621, the New Netherland Company was *superseded* by the West India Company, which established settlements (actually trading posts) on the Delaware and Connecticut Rivers, as well as at New Amsterdam and Fort Orange (now New York and Albany) on the Hudson River" (Reich 45).

The Dutch Parliament *chartered* the West India Company, a national-joint stock option company that would organize and oversee all Dutch ventures in the Western Hemisphere. The parliament *chartered* this new company in the hopes that it could encourage more private citizens to settle in the New World. To that end, in 1624, the West India Company sponsored 30 Dutch families, who established a settlement in present-day Manhattan. Even so, the Dutch pioneers were more interested in fur trade than in farming. By 1626, the struggling colony came under the administrative leadership of Director General Peter Minuit. Minuit is given credit for the now-famous purchase of Manhattan Island, approximately 22 acres, for 60 guilders (or $24) worth of trading goods. Manhattan, meaning "Island of Hills," was purchased from the Canarsie tribe (New York Historical Society Website).

Though progress was slow at best, the existence of the Dutch colony of New Netherland did not sit well with either the English or the Native American population. At one point during the 1630s, a small Dutch expedition sailed up the Connecticut River into an area that the English had already begun to settle. To avoid an armed conflict, the Dutch retreated; however, in doing so they forfeited the rights to the Connecticut River Valley.

Actually, the Dutch found conflict on every front. As noted earlier, the Dutch looked at the New World as an untapped "gold mine" in the form of rich fur trade, timber, and other commercial prospects. They struck an agreement or *appeasement* with the Iroquois *Confederacy* in an effort to preserve a peaceful coexistence. In essence, this appeasement granted concessions to the Iroquois, placing controls on trapping and fur trading. Though colonial leaders appeared to be vigilant, there was actually little enforcement of these policies, and corruption ran rampant throughout the settlement. In truth, the trade policies were a sham, and corruption and lax trade policies eroded the already *tenuous* relationship with the Iroquois *Confederacy*. Meanwhile, in the lower Hudson Valley, as more colonists began to set up small farms, the Dutch began to view Native Americans as an obstruction to their drive to expand their land claims. This sense of entitlement drove the Dutch to initiate a series of horrific campaigns against the region's Native American population through the 1630s and 1640s. Though the Dutch were successful in breaking the spirit and overall *solidarity* of the "River Indians," they also "managed to create a bitter atmosphere of tension and suspicion between European settlers and Native Americans" (nps.gov).

The West India Company continued to promote the settlement of New Netherland, eventually developing a land grant program whereby private citizens, referred to as patroons, were offered tracts of land stretching either 18 miles on one side of the Hudson River or 9 miles on each side, straddling the river. These patroons, who were in essence stockholders in the West India Company, in exchange for this land were expected to bring 50 settlers over the age of 15 to New Netherland within four years of receiving the grant. Patroons were to provide *tenants* with homes, cattle, and tools. In exchange, *tenants* paid rent to the patroon, had use of the patroon's mill, and were expected to maintain any roads and bridges on the estate (Reich 46).

In spite of the patroon program, immigration to New Netherland was slow at best. Few individuals took advantage of the patroon program as landowners, and even fewer settlers chose to participate as *tenants*. At that time, life in the Netherlands was so prosperous and religiously tolerant that few Dutch found the need even to consider a move to the North American continent. They were quite content with life in the Netherlands. "However, people from less fortunate areas of Europe settled in the Dutch colonies, and a report of 1643 indicates that eighteen different languages were spoken in New Amsterdam" (Reich 46). And though initially the West India Company mandated that all colonists be Calvinists, that rule was soon relaxed, as noted in the same 1643 report, which listed Catholics, Puritans, Lutherans, Anabaptists, and Mennonites worshipping in the Netherlands (Reich 46). By the 1650s, Quakers and Jews had also arrived in New Amsterdam to add to the religious mix.

In 1639, 10 years after instituting the ill-fated patroon program, the West India Company surrendered its *monopoly* of the fur trade, allowing all other businessmen to invest in New Netherland. In essence, all settlers would now be free to trade with the Native Americans. Profits increased as New Amsterdam enjoyed new economic activity. Food production, timber, tobacco, and eventually the slave trade all became a part of New Amsterdam's economy. Along with this period of relative prosperity came the negative aspects of unbridled economic growth, bribery, smuggling of taxable goods, and general lawlessness. In 1647, the Dutch West India Company, fearing these chaotic conditions could ultimately hurt its economic interests, appointed Peter Stuyvesant as Director General of New Netherland. Stuyvesant, who became known as "Hardhearted Pete," was a formidable figure. Stubborn, arrogant, and fitted with an ornately carved wooden leg, Stuyvesant heavy-handedly restored order to the colonies of New Netherland, issuing decrees, taking control of the management of taverns, and crippling much of the smuggling network that had become engrained in the daily operations of the colonies.

Though Stuyvesant was able to bring order to New Netherland during his 17-year tenure as director general, the Dutch and English had engaged in three naval wars over that same period of time. Among the battles, a major flashpoint occurred in 1663 off the West African coast. Here, the Dutch and British fought to protect their commercial interests, specifically in slaves, precious metals, and ivory. Though this dispute was recognized to be over slaves, ivory, and gold, it was also one in a series of demonstrations of naval power, for the Dutch and the English had been competing for European naval dominance for years.

The English had recognized the trading potential of the New Amsterdam site, and soon after the conflict off the West African coast, English warships sailed into New Amsterdam. Peter Stuyvesant found himself defenseless. He had no army to speak of, and no ships to engage in battle with the British fleet. He had no choice but to surrender without a fight. It was at this point that the English renamed New Amsterdam. They called it New York, in honor of James, Duke of York, the brother of King Charles of England, to whom the king had granted vast American territories, including New Amsterdam.

THE ENGLISH

In contrast to the colonization policies of Spain, France, and the Netherlands, immigration from England was not sponsored by the government. Rather, English migration was promoted by private groups, each with its own motives. Some came to gain religious freedom, while others came in hopes of working toward a better standard of living. Throughout the 16th century, wealthy land owners demanded higher rents from tenant farmers, often evicting those who could not pay. Eventually, as the *textile* industry grew in England, woolmaking became more profitable, resulting in many landlords evicting more tenant farmers to make more room for sheep. Though some tenant farmers moved to woodlands or upland areas to eke out an existence, many flocked to the towns and cities to find work. Wages were so poor that members of the working class could barely provide food and shelter for themselves. The gap widened between the wealthy, the landowners and merchants, and the working poor.

By the early 17th century, as the poor continued to migrate to towns in search of work, they often crossed paths with promoters offering packages to the New World. The packages usually offered free passage to North America in exchange for several years' labor as an *indentured* servant. Considering the poor living conditions of most in England at the time, many saw this opportunity of starting a new life in the New World as their only hope.

Jamestown

The first English colony to take hold in North America was Jamestown in 1607. Financed by the London Company, three small ships sailed into Chesapeake Bay and up a small waterway that the colonists named the James River in honor of their King. They called the settlement Jamestown, but in honor of their late virgin queen, they named the territory Virginia.

Virginia, its promoters hoped, would yield precious metals, or at the very least highly valued herbs and spices. Because of the misleading accounts of earlier explorers, settlers expected to find a land of "milk and honey." They were ill prepared for the demands of surviving in the wilderness. Of the band of 100 men and boys, about one in five were aristocrats, or gentlemen, who considered work beneath them. The other members of the *fledgling* colony were unskilled laborers, military recruits, and servants, none of whom had any idea of how to build a farming settlement. .

Supplies were mismanaged, and this problem was compounded by either an inability or an unwillingness to work productively at cultivating or hunting for food. Of the original 100 colonists, only 35 survived the first brutal year, and the survivors were on the brink of abandoning the settlement just as new settlers and supplies arrived.

Captain John Smith emerged as the leader of Jamestown colony. He brought order and discipline to the colony. Strict rules were enforced, even taken to extremes, with public hangings, floggings, and mutilations used as a means to force all to conform and to contribute to the common good of the settlement. The colony struggled for a full decade, but in 1611 the

Virginia Company began to grow tobacco, which quickly became a major source of *revenue* for the colony.

Massachusetts: Plymouth Colony

In 1620, 12 years after the establishment of Jamestown colony, a group of Christian reformers known as Pilgrims were beginning a new life north of Virginia, in present-day Massachusetts. This settlement was the first of what would be called the New England colonies. The Pilgrims onboard a small sailing ship, the *Mayflower*, were tossed about in a storm and thrown off course. Though they had sailed for Virginia, they landed on present-day Cape Cod. Believing that they were outside the *jurisdiction* of any organized government, the men drafted a formal agreement, which became known as the Mayflower *Compact*. This *compact*, which was based on democratic principles (government by the people), provided the Pilgrims with the framework for their own government as they formed a new religious society (Bigelow and Schmittroth 3).

In December (on Christmas Day), a month after their landing on Cape Cod, the *Mayflower* sailed into Plymouth Harbor. It was at Plymouth that the pilgrims built their settlement during the ensuing winter months. By April 1621, though half of their band of 100 men, women, and children had died of exposure and disease, the survivors moved off the *Mayflower* and onto solid ground, as portions of the settlement were inhabitable.

Had it not been for the help of the local Native Americans, it is likely that all of the Pilgrims would have perished during that first winter. Led by an English-speaking Native American, Samoset, members of the Wampanoag tribe taught the Pilgrims how to raise corn, or maize, and how to truly live off the land. The Pilgrims were very grateful for the help, and gave thanks. They invited Massasoit, chief of the Wampanoag Confederacy, and 90 of his braves to a three-day feast. Among the main dishes served at this feast were deer meat and turkey, a large *indigenous* fowl new to the English settlers. Plymouth remained an independent colony until 1691, when it was annexed by Massachusetts.

Massachusetts Bay Colony

The relative success of Plymouth colony spurred another religious group, the Puritans, to come to New England and establish the Massachusetts Bay Colony. In 1628, a group of Puritan merchants formed the Company of New England, sending a group of settlers to Salem. There were two major factors motivating the Puritans to seek a new life in America. First, they were facing *persecution*, as the archbishop of the Anglican Church had ordered that all churches in England follow the dictates of the Church of England, and, second, a depression of the textile industry had brought great economic distress to the southern and eastern counties of England, where the majority of Puritans lived (Reich 77).

One year later, in 1629, the Company of New England secured a new charter from Charles I and changed its name to the Massachusetts Bay Company. John Winthrop, an East Anglican gentleman who had received his legal education at Cambridge, became the leader of the colony. Winthrop had held a royal judicial past, and was a substantial landowner in Suffolk County (Reich 77). However, by the late 1620s, he found himself out of office and deeply in debt. His strong religious *conviction*, coupled with England's prohibition of Puritan religious practices, gave him the impetus to settle in America. But Winthrop established the Massachusetts Bay Company with a different set of ground rules. First, Winthrop persuaded those stockholders of the Massachusetts Bay Company who were not interested in settling in America to sell their interests in the company to Winthrop and 11 other committed Puritans. Of particular interest was the company's charter, which granted it political and economic rights in New England and, most unusual at the time, failed to require that the company meetings be held in England. This freed Winthrop and his disciples to truly govern their own affairs. With these fundamental pieces in place, Winthrop set sail in 1630 with 11 sailing vessels carrying 700 settlers, 240 cows, and 60 horses. Another feature unique to the Massachusetts Bay Colony was that the Puritan settlers accompanying Winthrop were family groups, as opposed to just men interested in adventure and the potential for financial gain.

Winthrop's dream was to create a "city upon a hill," by which he meant a place where Puritans could live in strict accordance with their religious beliefs (usinfo.org). Because of his attention to detail in the preparation and planning of the colony, Massachusetts' population grew within a decade to almost 20,000. Winthrop established Boston as the colony's hub, along with a ring of towns around it (Clark and Hewitt 46). These included small fishing camps that quickly grew into the towns of Gloucester, Salem, and Marblehead.

The original charter granted in 1629 remained the colony's legal foundation for 55 years, until 1684. Winthrop and his Puritan colleagues soon collaborated with the Pilgrims and Plymouth Colony, though Plymouth Colony remained separate until 1691.

Rhode Island

As their numbers grew, the Puritan colonists spread to the west and south in particular. A major dispute between the strict Puritan Church and a young clergyman, Roger Williams, led to his *banishment* from the Massachusetts Bay Colony. Williams established a colony in nearby Rhode Island, which soon became a haven for those who wanted to escape the rigid rules and practices of the Puritan Church. In 1636, Roger Williams purchased land from the Narragansett Indians in present-day Providence. To his credit, Williams set up the first American colony where complete separation of church and state as well as freedom of religion was practiced (usinfo.org).

By the mid-1630s, others who found it difficult to live under the *precepts* of the Puritan Church began to leave the Massachusetts Bay Colony. The fertile soil of the Connecticut River Valley attracted many who had a farming interest, including migrants from Plymouth. Outbreaks of smallpox in 1633, which devastated Native American tribes in these areas, made this migration by English settlers that much easier, as they confronted little resistance from the Native Americans in the area. Soon the colonies of Connecticut and New Haven were established, with settlements also cropping up along the New Hampshire and Maine coasts.

Maryland

Further to the south, the first propriety colony, Maryland, was founded. Whereas the New England colonies were under the jurisdiction of the Puritan Church, the southern colonies were given to British aristocrats by the king. In 1632, Lord Baltimore (George Calvert), leading the Calvert family, obtained a charter from King Charles I for land north of the Potomac River. Since the charter did not explicitly prohibit the establishment of non-Protestant churches, the Calvert family encouraged fellow Catholics to settle there.

George Calvert had served as a member of Parliament until his conversion to Catholicism ruined his political career. Calvert, Lord Baltimore, financed this fledgling colony almost completely out of his own pocket (Reich 68). Maryland's first town was St. Mary's, established in 1634 near where the Potomac flows into the Chesapeake Bay.

While establishing the refuge for Catholics who were facing increasing persecution in Anglican England, the Calvert family was also committed to creating profitable estates. To attain their goal, and to appease the British government, they also encouraged Protestants to settle in Maryland.

Carolina

Following suit, in 1670 Carolina became the next *proprietary* colony, owned by a consortium of eight proprietors. The two parts, north and south, developed differently, with the south establishing large rice plantations utilizing slave labor and the north focusing on the cultivation of tobacco. In 1712, the northern part became a separate colony.

Georgia

Georgia became the last of the *proprietary* colonies, with its grant going to a group of British philanthropists. Their mission was to provide debtors with an opportunity to start a new life. The philanthropic trustees of Georgia colony embraced various idealistic schools of thought and imposed them on the citizenry. These ideals included no alcohol, no large estates, and no slavery. The prohibition on slavery led to Georgia's less prosperous start in comparison to its northern neighbors.

Though restrictive *idealism* held back Georgia's growth, another form of idealism made another proprietary colony, Pennsylvania, extremely prosperous.

Pennsylvania

Pennsylvania, granted to William Penn in 1681, was founded on the principle of freedom of conscience. William Penn was the son of Admiral Penn, a longtime friend of Charles II. The young Penn, much to his father's surprise, was jailed for attending a Quaker meeting in 1667. At the time, the Quakers were regarded as one of the most radical groups in England. Penn, however, through his involvement with the Quakers, found a lifelong commitment to religious liberty. As a result of a sizeable loan that the senior Penn had made to Charles II, William Penn was able to gain what he saw as an extraordinary, God-given opportunity to conduct a "holy experiment" in America. Upon his father's death, William accepted the grant of a tract of land in America in 1681, as discharge of the royal debt. The king granted Penn a charter to Pennsylvania—the largest land charter ever made to one individual (Reich 95).

Penn named the new colony Pennsylvania, or Penn's woodlands, in honor of his father. Along with Quakers, Penn encouraged Mennonites, Amish, Moravians, and Baptists to join him in settling Pennsylvania. Colonists settling in Pennsylvania were expected to believe in one God, the creator of the universe, but that was the limit of required religious conformity. Penn proclaimed his commitment to religious tolerance through his Charter of Liberties, drafted in 1701, which stated,

> *No person . . . who shall confers1 and acknowledges One Almighty God . . . and profess him . . . shall be in any case molested or prejudiced . . . because of his . . . Persuasion or Practice. (Reich 95)*

Also, in keeping with his faith, Penn was motivated by a sense of equality not often found in other American colonies at that time. Hence, women in Pennsylvania had rights long before they did in other parts of America.

Like Roger Williams, Penn also acknowledged that the Native Americans were the rightful owners of the land and that he would have to purchase the land from them so as to legitimize his ownership. In that vein, beginning in 1682 he conducted a series of meetings with the Delaware Indians, who sold much of their land to him in exchange for protection from the Iroquois.

Penn undertook a comprehensive advertising campaign all over Europe in an effort to bring settlers to Pennsylvania. Upon his arrival in Pennsylvania he found a few Dutch and Swedish settlers living along the Delaware River, but soon large numbers of Quakers from England and Wales migrated to Pennsylvania. Among the impoverished and persecuted across Europe, an appreciable number of Germans responded to Penn's solicitations and soon made passage to America, settling in Pennsylvania. Within a few years of its founding, Pennsylvania's population had already climbed to 12,000. Penn had meticulously drawn up plans for the city of Philadelphia, positioning it at the confluence of the Delaware and Schuylkill Rivers.

Penn named the territory's main settlement the "City of Brotherly Love" in deference to his strong moral and ethical convictions. Coupling its strategic position as a major import and export center with its large numbers of immigrants, Philadelphia soon became the capital of Pennsylvania, as well as one of the most important and prosperous cities in the colonies.

Keywords and Terms

1. appeasement
2. autocratic
3. anishment
4. campaigns
5. chartered
6. commissioned
7. compact
8. confederacy
9. converting
10. conviction
11. dominate
12. edicts
13. elusive
14. fledgling
15. idealism
16. indentured
17. indigenous
18. jurisdiction
19. missionaries
20. monopoly
21. municipal council
22. penetrated

23. persecution
24. precarious
25. precepts
26. proprietary
27. quest
28. revenue
29. solidarity
30. superseded
31. tenants
32. tenuous
33. textile
34. ventures
35. vied
36. vigilant

BIBLIOGRAPHY

Bigelow, Barbara, and Linda Schmittroth. *American Revolution Almanac.* Boston: UXL–Gale Group, 2000.

Clark, Christopher, Nancy Hewitt, Joshua Brown, and David Jaffee. *Who Built America?* Boston: Bedford/ St. Martin's, 2000.

"Dutch Colonies." nps.gov. National Park Service, 12/8/2009. March 2, 2012. <www.nps.gov/nr/travel/ kingston/colonization.htm>.

"New York: History." *Islands Draw Native American, Dutch, and English Settlement.* New York Histori-cal Society, n.d. February 28, 2012. <www.city-data.com/us-cities/The-Northeast/New-York-History.html>.

Polk, William R. *The Birth of America.* New York: HarperCollins, 2006.

Reich, Jerome R. *Colonial America.* Upper Saddle River, NJ: Prentice Hall, 2001.

8

English and Dutch Colonists: Book 1

Title: *Outlaw*
Author: Angus Donald
Grade/Age: Young Adult
ISBN: 9780312678364
NCSS Standards: 1,2,3,4,5,6,8

ANNOTATION

The life of young Alan Dale, Robin Hood's trusted right-hand man, is revealed in this late 12th-century novel set primarily in Sherwood Forest. Robin is a ruthless man who cannot be trusted and the band of outlaws consists of some of the most notorious thieves and murderers in England.

SUGGESTED VOCABULARY

adder, aketon, alewife, apprentice, atrocities, belligerence, bow staves, burins, cavalcade, cernunnos, chevrons, conroi, cudgel, demesne, desecrate, destitute, docile, dovecote, earldom, euphoria, gawped, hamlet, infidels, intemperate, largesse, lintel, mace, malleable, mallet, mare, mirth, morass, outlaw, pagans, penance, raucous, retinue, reverent, reveres, ruffian, ruse, scabbard, sodden, supplicants, surcoat, surreptitiously, swathe, tithes, touvere

BEFORE READING: PREPARING TO JUMP INTO THE BOOK

Depicting Words through Art

Each student chooses two words from the suggested vocabulary and depicts those words through one of the following art forms: drawing, clay, video, music, dance, painting, or photography. Students define the word and then "depict" that word for their classmates through the two media in which they are most comfortable.

Investigating the Middle Ages

Students are placed in groups of four or five to work as a team of investigators. Each team is given a "case" to investigate. Their task is to compile of list of 20 facts for their case from three different reputable sources. One source should be the school library's history database. They must also organize their facts into a PowerPoint presentation that includes at least five illustrations or photographs. Once the presentations are compiled, the teams will present their findings to the class in an oral presentation using the PowerPoint presentation as their notes of the case. Distribute the Case File Handout in Figure 8.1. Students can also be assessed on their presentation of material using the PowerPoint Presentation Rubric found in Figure 8.2. Case topics might include music and instruments of the Middle Ages, the legend of Robin Hood, weapons and warfare of the Middle Ages, people of the Middle Ages, women in the Middle Ages, religion in the Middle Ages, and sports/entertainment of the Middle Ages.

Making a Sundial

Invite students to make a virtual sundial at <http://www.gcstudio.com/makedial.html> and research the use of sundials. Then, require students to work with a partner to create one of the six sundial projects found on the website <http://www.sundials.co.uk/projects.htm>.

Interpreting a Ballad

Students read and listen to a ballad about Robin Hood at <http://www.boldoutlaw.com/ rhbal/bal139.html> and write a two-page reaction to and interpretation of the work. Students who feel so inclined could listen to several ballads to get multiple interpretations.

DURING READING: GUIDED DISCUSSION QUESTIONS

1. Describe the narrator's mood in Chapter 1. What has happened to him?
2. Why does the narrator (Alan) tell Robin Hood's story?
3. Explain why Alan is forced to become a thief.
4. Who is Sir Ralph Murdoc? Describe his physical features. Why should he be feared?
5. If caught, Alan would have to face terrible consequences for stealing. What are the consequences? How did you react to learning this information?
6. Alan's mother takes him to see someone. Who does she take him to see and why?
7. Describe how Alan's father died.
8. Describe Robin Hood.
9. What was Alan's penance for stealing? How does his mother feel? How would you feel if you were Alan?
10. Describe Tuck. Do you like him? Why or why not?
11. Describe Alan's first day with Robin Hood.
12. How did Tuck and Robin Hood come to know each other?
13. Why did Tuck's "gluttony" need to be cured?
14. Why does Alan cry when he delivers Robin's dinner at the end of Chapter 2?
15. On page 36, the narrator meets a woman in Robin's chambers. Describe the woman. Who is she?
16. Robin convinces Alan to avenge his father's death. How do you think he will do this?
17. Why are outlaws known as "wolf heads"? What is the significance of the term?
18. Describe the fight in Chapter 3. How does Alan react? How would you react?
19. In Chapter 4, Alan feels victory. How does this make him feel? Find a quote from the chapter to support your answer.
20. Describe Thangbrand's Hall. Would you enjoy living there? Why or why not?
21. What does Alan see when he visits Thangbrand's quarters?
22. Why do they call Thangbrand the "Widow Maker?"
23. At the end of Chapter 4, Alan finally realizes what he wants to do with his life. What is it?

Case File Handout

Facts:

1. _____   11. _____

2. _____   12. _____

3. _____   13. _____

4. _____   14. _____

5. _____   15. _____

6. _____   16. _____

7. _____   17. _____

8. _____   18. _____

9. _____   19. _____

10. _____   20. _____

Sources:

1.

2.

3.

Figure 8.1: Case File Handout

PowerPoint Presentation Rubric

Criteria	4	3	2	1
Content	Content was a highly comprehensive argument that included evidence from newspaper.	Content was organized with somewhat meaningful statements from newspaper.	Content was unorganized but used some statements from newspaper.	Content was unorganized with no supporting evidence from newspaper.
Organization	Student was highly organized in not reading from presentation or using notes.			Student was very unorganized in not having presentation or note cards.
Speaking	Student spoke enthusiastically during presentation.		Student mumbled during presentation.	Student refused to present project.
Time Management	Student spoke within allotted time.	Student exceeded allotted time by one minute.	Student exceeded allotted time by two minutes.	Student exceeded allotted time by three minutes or did not speak.
PowerPoint Presentation	Student was effective in delivering PowerPoint presentation by meeting all requirements.		Student completed PowerPoint presentation with some requirements.	Student did not complete PowerPoint presentation.

Total _____/ 20 points

Comments:

Figure 8.2: PowerPoint Presentation Rubric

From *Beyond the Textbook: Using Trade Books and Databases to Teach Our Nation's History, Grades 7–12* by Carianne Bernadowski, Robert Del Greco, and Patricia L. Kolencik. Santa Barbara, CA: Libraries Unlimited. Copyright © 2013.

24. Describe Bernard. What is his job? Describe the relationship between Bernard and Alan.
25. Describe Guy. Do you like him? Why or why not?
26. Who is the Lord of Sherwood?
27. Why do you think Robin wants to take Alan to Nottingham in Chapter 5?
28. What happens in the tavern?
29. Describe Sherwood in autumn.
30. Why is Sir Richard leaving Thangbrand's?
31. What gift does Sir Richard give Alan before he leaves?
32. In Chapter 9, we learn of Alan's mother's death. How does he react?
33. At the beginning of Chapter 10, Robin returns. How does Alan react? Why?
34. What is "The Death Song of the Sherwood Werewolf"?
35. Describe Alan's first council of war with Robin's men at the Caves.
36. Why does Tuck leave Robin's cave?
37. Describe the job of the home-loving birds.
38. Describe the people who follow the doves to Robin's cave.
39. What is the ritual performed on Piers? Why was he being punished?
40. Why did Robin send Alan away? How did it make him feel? Where did he go?
41. Robin gives Alan a gift. What was it?
42. Who accompanies Alan to Winchester?
43. Describe Winchester Castle.
44. Why does Alan feel like an imposter at Winchester Castle? Is he one?
45. On page 235, the text reads "panic is a great enemy." What does this line mean? Describe a time in your life when it might have applied.
46. Describe how Alan is punished in the castle after Guy reveals his identity. How did it make you feel?
47. Describe Maria-Anne's rescue. What did you expect to happen?
48. In Chapter 17, Alan describes the battle from memory. Do you think his account is accurate? Why or why not?
49. In Chapter 18, why do you think Robin asks Alan to release a white dove?
50. Describe Robin and Alan's attack on Sir Murdoc.
51. What does Alan finally reveal to Guy during their sword fight?
52. How does Robin become Earl Robert?
53. Robin learns that Hugh betrayed him. Do does Robin react? How would you react?
54. How did you react to the ending of the book? Tell a friend.

AFTER READING: CONNECTING TO THE TEXT

Writing a Wedding Invitation

Require students to work in pairs to create the perfect wedding invitation to Robin Hood and Maria's wedding. Since Maria is royalty, the invitation should be grand, yet reflect both of their personalities. Students can create the invitation by hand on oaktag and other materials such as ribbon, or on the computer using Microsoft Word.

Epitaph for Robin Hood

Require students to write an epitaph for Robin Hood. They should be careful to create an epitaph that reflects his personality. Students should pay special attention to creating an overall polished piece of work. Classroom teachers and school librarians can use the epitaph rubric found at <http://www.docstoc.com/docs/24334439/Epitaph-Rubric> for assessment purposes.

Book Jacket

Review the cover of the current book with students and ask questions about the title, illustration, use of color, general significance, and other relevant questions. Students can connect the text to the importance of the cover. Ask students to imagine that they work at a large publishing house and the author has asked for a new cover for the newest edition of the book. Require students to work with a partner as a creative team to create the perfect book cover for the release of the new book. Students should first consider the target audience and purpose of the new cover. Questions to consider:

- Does it need to have a larger teen appeal?
- What does the current cover do to convey the meaning of the book?
- What does the current book cover not do?
- Should a book cover be symbolic in some way?
- Should text be included on a book cover aside from the title and author?
- Should the book cover be in color, black and white, or limited color for effect?
- Will students use photographs, graphics, illustrations, or simply words?

Students should recognize that the purpose of the book cover is to grab potential readers' attention. After students have created the concept for the cover, they should create a rough draft of their idea. Students can simply do this on a plain sheet of paper. In addition to the front cover, students should create a summary for the inside cover consisting of 150–200 words. The back of the book should contain the author's biography on the inside flap. On the back cover students write a review of the book in their own words. They can rate the book using a four-star system (one meaning poor and four meaning excellent) with an explanation. Use the Book Jacket Rubric in Figure 8.3 for assessment purposes.

Bulletin Board

Compare and contrast Robin Hood and Little John using the Compare and Contrast Matrix found in Figure 8.4. Students must list 10 attributes for which they will list the similarities and differences. Once they list the attributes in column one, they then check or place an X under each character's name. Students then create a "mock" bulletin board depicting the similarities and differences between the two characters. The mock bulletin board should be completed on an 8 1/2 x 11 sheet of plain white paper. Students vote on the best bulletin board, which will be displayed in the classroom or library.

DIGGING INTO THE DATABASE

Outlaws

Although it is still debated if Robin Hood indeed existed, he was considered one of the world's most notorious outlaws. Students use the school library's history database to research other notorious outlaws from history. Students then create a puppet of their outlaw and a 10-minute speech written in first person. The rest of the class has to guess who the notorious outlaw is by the description and the puppet.

Book Jacket Rubric

Criteria	2	1	0
Front Cover	The cover is highly creative and vividly depicts the story through quality pictures and/or drawings. Title, author, and publisher are present.	The cover is creative and depicts the story. Some pictures or drawings aren't as neat as they could be. The title, author, or publisher is missing.	The cover does not depict the story OR two of the required elements are missing.
Inside Cover (flap)	The summary of the story is accurate, well written, and 150–200 words in length.	The summary is accurate but not 150–200 words in length.	The summary is inaccurate AND not 150–200 words in length.
Back Cover (flap)	Author's biography is highly accurate and well written with no grammatical errors.	Author's biography is accurate but contains 1–2 grammatical errors.	Author's biography is inaccurate OR contains 3 or more grammatical errors.
Back Cover	Extremely well-written, accurate summary and rating with no grammatical errors.	Accurate summary and rating but contains 1–2 grammatical errors.	Either the summary or rating is missing OR it contains 3 or more grammatical errors.

Figure 8.3: Book Jacket Rubric

From *Beyond the Textbook: Using Trade Books and Databases to Teach Our Nation's History, Grades 7–12* by Carianne Bernadowski, Robert Del Greco, and Patricia L. Kolencik. Santa Barbara, CA: Libraries Unlimited. Copyright © 2013

Compare and Contrast Matrix

	Robin Hood	Little John
Attribute 1		
Attribute 2		
Attribute 3		
Attribute 4		
Attribute 5		
Attribute 6		
Attribute 7		
Attribute 8		
Attribute 9		
Attribute 10		

Figure 8.4: Compare and Contrast Matrix

From *Beyond the Textbook: Using Trade Books and Databases to Teach Our Nation's History, Grades 7–12* by Carianne Bernadowski, Robert Del Greco, and Patricia L. Kolencik. Santa Barbara, CA: Libraries Unlimited. Copyright © 2013.

Previewing the Text

Subtitle	Subtitle	Subtitle	Subtitle
*	*	*	*
*	*	*	*
*	*	*	*
*	*	*	*
*	*	*	*
*	*	*	*
*	*	*	*
*	*	*	*
*	*	*	*
*	*	*	*
*	*	*	*
*	*	*	*
*	*	*	*
*	*	*	*
*	*	*	*
*	*	*	*
*	*	*	*
*	*	*	*
*	*	*	*
*	*	*	*
*	*	*	*
*	*	*	*
*	*	*	*
*	*	*	*
*	*	*	*
*	*	*	*
*	*	*	*
*	*	*	*

Figure 8.5: Previewing the Text

Medieval Castle

Students work with a partner or small group to create a three-dimensional depiction of a medieval castle. Students can use clay or other materials to build their castles. Students can use descriptions or pictures found either on the internet or in the school library's history and / or art databases.

Magna Carta

Students read an article about the Magna Carta accessed from the school library's history database or the internet. School librarians and classroom teachers should find an article that best meets their students' reading levels. Before reading, distribute the Previewing the Text found in Figure 8.5. Students should first look at the title and subtitles and predict what they might learn. Students then read the Magna Carta and take notes under the appropriate subtitles they have created. Finally, they place a star next to any law they believe Robin Hood would break and explain why they think this is so.

Comparing Weapons

Students use the school library's history database to investigate weapons that may have been used during the time that Robin Hood may have lived. Students choose two weapons to illustrate and describe to the class.

READ ALIKES

Bows against the Barons by Geoffrey Trease ISBN 9781904027263 (Ages 9–12)

Child of the May by Theresa Tomlinson ISBN 9781841620640 (Young Adult/Adult)

The Chronicles of Robin Hood by Rosemary Sutcliff ISBN 9783772518713 (Young Adult/Adult)

Forestwife by Theresa Tomlinson ISBN 9780440913108 (Young Adult/Adult)

Holy Warrior: A Novel of Robin Hood by Angus Donald ISBN9780312678371 (Young Adult/Adult)

In a Dark Wood by Michael Cadnum ISBN 9780141306384 (Young Adult/Adult)

The Outlaws of Sherwood by Robin McKinley ISBN9780441013258 (Young Adult/Adult)

Robin's Country by Monica Furlong ISBN 9780679890997 (Ages 9–12)

Rowan Hood by Nancy Springer ISBN 9780698119727 (Young Adult/Adult)

Sherwood: A Collection of Original Robin Hood Stories by Jane Yolen ISBN 9780399231827 (Ages 9–12)

9

English and Dutch Colonists: Book 2

Title: *Out of Many Waters*
Author: Jacqueline Dembar Greene
Grade/Age: 5–8
ISBN: 9780595380473
NCSS Standards: 1,2,3,4,5,6,8

ANNOTATION

Twelve-year-old Isobel and her sister Maria are kidnapped and taken to a monastery in Brazil. Readers learn the horrors and the harsh treatment the girls encounter, and Maria eventually insists they must run away to Amsterdam. The girls board different ships and the despicable treatment does not end. Eventually, Isobel finds family and comfort on the ship and safely arrives in New Amsterdam, hoping that someday she will be reunited with her family.

SUGGESTED VOCABULARY

admonish, banter, berimbaos, bodice, brusquely, caravel, challah bread, chemise, chided, convert, corpulent, derisive, disobedient, dispel, docile, embroidered, fervently, foremast, fortnight, frock, furtively, guilder, helmsman, immigrants, imperious, infidel, Inquisition, modesty, monastery, natives, ominously, optimistic, pirates, portends, privateers, pungent, resignation, Rosh Hashanah, Sabbath, sabotage, sacrilege, scabbard, Shabbat, shrewd, smug, stockade, stomacher, stowaways, Torah, translator, trepidation, trough

BEFORE READING: PREPARING TO JUMP INTO THE BOOK

Vocabulary Application

Distribute the Vocabulary Application in Figure 9.1 to students. Students then work in pairs to investigate the vocabulary terms. First, students define the word in their own words and write it in the space provided. Next, they find friends and ask them to supply a definition. Then, students find the definition from a primary source. Finally, they draw an illustration to demonstrate understanding.

Vocabulary Application

Word	My Definition	Friend's Definition	Primary Source Definition	Illustration (in space provided or attached)
Monastery				
Infidel				
Frock				
Stowaways				
Helmsman				
Immigrants				
Pirate				
Trepidation				

Figure 9.1: Vocabulary Application

Jewish Community Visitor

Invite a member of the Jewish community to speak to students about topics they will learn about in the book, such as the Torah, Rosh Hashanah, Sabbath, and Shabbat. Students can then ask clarifying questions and have a working knowledge of the concepts they will encounter in the text.

Jewish Food Festival

Ask students to find Jewish food recipes that they would like to try. Allow students to vote on the top five and prepare recipes for a mini "food festival" in the classroom or school library.

Writing Your Bio

Students should visit <http://www.jdgbooks.com/meet_jackie.htm> to read the biography of author Jacqueline Dembar. Once students read about her life, they should begin brainstorming the important events in their own lives. Students then write their own biographies as if they had websites similar to Jacqueline Dembar's website. Once students compose their biographies, they can type their work using a word processing program and post them, along with a picture, on the bulletin board or school library display case. A biography rubric can be found at <http://teacherweb.com/CO/FrontierCharterAcademy/FifthSixth/biogra phyrubric.pdf>.

DURING READING: GUIDED DISCUSSION QUESTIONS

1. Where do you think Isobel and Maria are going at the beginning of the book?
2. What happens to Jewish people who refuse to convert?
3. Why was Isobel taken from her family?
4. What do you think Maria's plan will be in Chapter 1?
5. Describe Padre Diego and Padre Francisco. Do you like the men? Why or why not?
6. What is a friar?
7. Why are the friars in a rush to get to the colonies?
8. What do the friars consider an infidel religion? Why do you think this is so?
9. At the end of Chapter 1, Maria states, "My plan has to succeed!" (p. 8). Why do you think she says this?
10. How does Recife differ from the monastery?
11. Why do you think Maria needs the eggs so badly in Chapter 2? Explain why the girls must boil the eggs.
12. Describe Maria's plan to escape. How does Isobel react? How would you react?
13. On page 21, we learn that the girls lived in Portugal with their parents before going with the friars. How did the girls end up with the friars?
14. Why do they want to go to Amsterdam?
15. Explain the quote on page 23: "I was a child when I stepped onto that boat. But I became a woman as soon as it sailed, for there was no more time to be a little girl."
16. Why does Maria become upset when Isobel eats the bacon that Padre serves with breakfast? Would you have eaten the bacon? Why or why not?
17. Why do you think Padre allows Isobel to board the ship at the end of Chapter 4?
18. Describe Isobel's hiding place on the ship.

19. At the end of Chapter 5, the boat is finally sailing. What do you predict will happen?
20. Explain what happens to Isobel's food and water on the boat.
21. Who do you think leaves water and cheese next to the longboat for Isobel?
22. Describe the Spaniards' conversation on the boat.
23. While on the boat, what does Isobel learn about the whistle?
24. How is Isobel discovered under the longboat?
25. Describe Maria Levy.
26. What does Isobel mean when she says "arrange my passage" on page 70?
27. Who is Paulo? How does he help Isobel? Predict how she might repay him in the future.
28. Describe Rochelle. Do you like her? Why or why not?
29. What do the families on the boat offer to do for Isobel? Why?
30. At the beginning of Chapter 10, Isobel is desperate to speak to the captain. Why?
31. Why do you think Isobel wants to work for the captain?
32. Describe Cado.
33. Why does Isobel think the helmsman is part of a master plan?
34. Explain Davy's kindness to Isobel on page 96.
35. Describe the Sabbath ceremony.
36. Why does Isobel not want to learn Hebrew? Do you think she will regret this decision?
37. Why is Isobel jealous of Rochelle? Why is Rochelle jealous of Isobel?
38. What does the helmsman plan to do to the Jews on the boat? How does this make you feel?
39. What happens when the Spanish privateers board Isobel's boat?
40. Why does Cado make Isobel change her clothes at the beginning of Chapter 13?
41. Why does Isobel have to pretend to not know Maria Levy and her family? Would you have done the same?
42. Why do the privateers plan to turn the Jews over to the Inquisition? What does that mean for their future?
43. Why do you think the privateers take the Jews to Cuba?
44. Describe the conditions for the Jews in Cuba.
45. Why does Isobel feel responsible for the Jewish people's captivity?
46. Why does Isobel teach the children to read? Describe the benefits to the children. Describe the benefits to Isobel.
47. What does Isobel think will happen when they arrive in Madrid?
48. What does Davy teach Isobel?
49. Describe how the relationship between Isobel and Rochelle has changed throughout the book.
50. Why is Isobel disappointed when she learns they will go to New Amsterdam? How does this change her plans?
51. Describe the relationship between Isobel and Maria Levy. Why is Maria so important to Isobel?
52. What is the significance of Isobel's dream, described on page 175?
53. Paulo reads from the Bible. Describe the reactions of the onlookers.
54. The Jews must pay their passage when they arrive in New Amsterdam. What will happen if they cannot pay? How do you think they can get money for payment?
55. What does Isobel do with her combs? Would you have done the same? Why or why not?

AFTER READING: CONNECTING TO THE TEXT

Writing to Maria

Students write a letter to Maria from Isobel. Students should first decide on the point in the book at which they will write the letter. The letter should include important incidents that occurred throughout Isobel's journey.

Writing a New Ending

Students work in pairs or small groups to write a new ending to the book. Students should first write a rough draft and then spend time peer-editing and revising before a final draft is created. Allow students to type their endings on a word processing program to share with the class or hang in the school library for display. Classroom teachers and/or school librarians can use the Story Ending Rubric found in Figure 9.2 for assessment purposes.

Writing a Comparison Essay

Students compare Isobel and one other character of their choice to write a comparison essay. First, students should use the Venn diagram in Figure 9.3 to compare and contrast the physical and personality traits of Isobel and their chosen character. Then, students can write an essay to compare the two characters.

DIGGING INTO THE DATABASE

Timeline

Students work in pairs or small groups to create a timeline that leads up to 1654, when Isobel was first kidnapped. Students use a history database to search for information that will help them piece together the historical milestones that occurred before and during that time period. Once students find sufficient information, they can create their timeline on the computer or on poster board.

Responding to Artwork

Students search for a photograph that illustrates surrender of New Amsterdam. Students can use the history database in the school library. Classroom teachers and/or school librarians can use a document camera or smartboard to display the photograph for the entire class to view. Classroom teachers and/or school librarians can ask students the following questions:

- Why is this photograph important to Isobel's journey in the book?
- What do you see in the photo?
- Who do we see? (Be sure the students can see all parts of the illustration clearly.)
- How are the people responding?
- Why are some people looking out into the water? What do they see?
- What do you think the woman is doing? Why?

Next, give each student a copy of the photograph and ask them to write a caption. They may choose to include dialogue if they wish. Finally, students should share their captions and explain why they wrote that particular caption.

Story Ending Rubric

Criteria	3	2	1
Problem/Solution	The writers include a distinct problem and solution.	The writers include either a problem or solution.	The writers do not include a problem and solution.
Logical Ending	The writers include a logical ending to the story.	The writers include an ending to the story.	The writers do not include a logical ending to the story.
Relationship to Story	There is a clear relationship to the story.	The relationship to the story is somewhat unclear.	There is no relationship to the story.
Capitalization/ Punctuation	There are no errors in capitalization and/or punctuation.	There is one error in either capitalization and/or punctuation.	There are two or more errors in capitalization and/ or punctuation.
Spelling	There are no errors in spelling.	There is one error in spelling.	There are two or more errors in spelling.

Figure 9.2: Story Ending Rubric

From *Beyond the Textbook: Using Trade Books and Databases to Teach Our Nation's History, Grades 7–12* by Carianne Bernadowski, Robert Del Greco, and Patricia L. Kolencik. Santa Barbara, CA: Libraries Unlimited. Copyright © 2013.

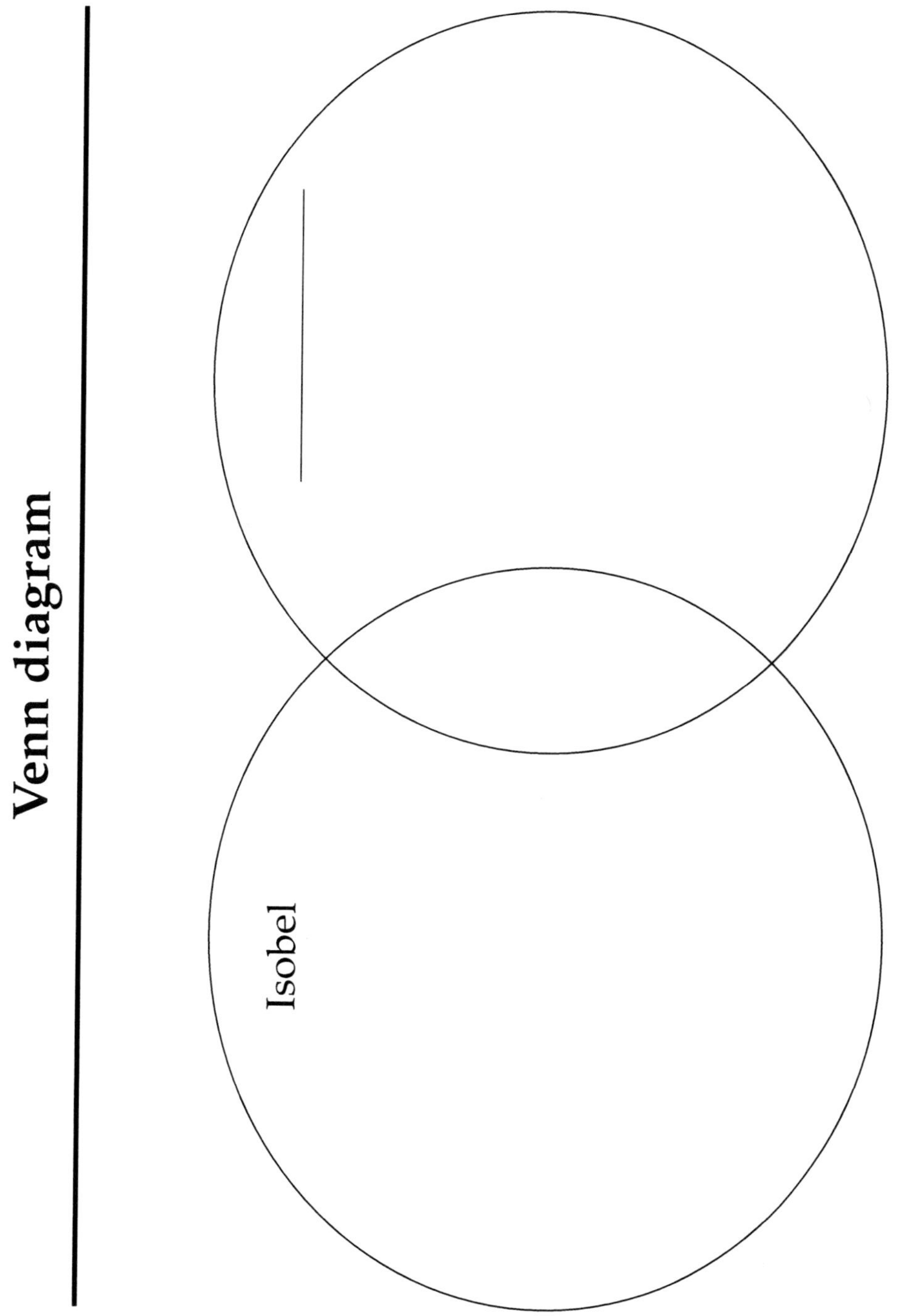

Venn diagram

Isobel

Figure 9.3: Venn Diagram

Fact Finder

Category	Facts
Example: Food	

Figure 9.4: Fact Finder

New Amsterdam Modernized

Students work in pairs or small groups to write a modern-day dialogue between Isobel and Rochelle when they arrive at New Amsterdam. Since New Amsterdam later became New York City, use a history database to research the sights and sounds of New York City today. If Isobel and Rochelle were landing in New York City, what might they say and do differently?

Life on a Ship

For much of the story, Isobel is living on a ship. Research the living conditions on a ship during the 1600s, including the threat of disease, living quarters, and the threat of pirates. Students can use the school library database as a resource. Students use the Fact Finder in Figure 9.4 to gather the information. Students then share the information with the class to enhance comprehension of the book.

READ ALIKES

Bridge by Karen Hesse ISBN 9780312378868 (Young Adult/Adult)

The Castle on Hester Street by Linda Heller ISBN 0689874340 (Young Adult/Adult)

The Inheritance by Claudia Von Canon ISBN 9780395338919 (Young Adult/Adult)

The Iron Peacock by Mary Stetson Clarke ISBN 9781887840675 (Young Adult/Adult)

Journey to the Golden Land by Richard Rosenblum ISBN 082760405X (Young Adult/Adult)

The Keeping Quilt by Patricia Polacco ISBN 0689844476 (Ages 9–12)

The King of Mulberry Street by Donna Jo Napoli ISBN 0385746539 (Young Adult/Adult)

One Foot Ashore by Jacqueline Dembar Greene ISBN 0802776019 (Young Adult/Adult)

Stowaway by Karen Hesse ISBN 9780689839894 (Young Adult/Adult)

When Jessie Came across the Sea by Amy Hest ISBN 076361274X (Young Adult/Adult)

10

The American Revolution: An Introduction to Teaching This Time Period

PRE-REVOLUTIONARY PERIOD

Seven Years' War

The Seven Years' War, or the French and Indian War, was ultimately a contest between France and England, with control of North America and India as the prize. Conflict between the French and the British had been brewing for decades, and by the 1740s *skirmishes* continued, as the two colonial empires wrestled over land, sea ports, and trading rights. The Hudson Bay Company expanded its activities into upper New York and the Great Lakes, while the boundaries of Nova Scotia were still in dispute. The two countries also disputed the ownership of the islands of St. Lucia and Tobago in the Caribbean, with both countries laying claim to them. But the tipping point occurred when a Pennsylvania trader, Conrad Weiser, negotiated a major fur trading agreement with the Miami tribe, which had moved into the Ohio Valley in 1748 (Reich 269). This agreement, known as the Logstown Treaty, mandated that Native Americans trade fur exclusively with Pennsylvania traders, not with the French. This pact had the potential to cripple the Canadian economy, and the French saw the English commitment to settling in the Ohio Valley as a threat to the lines of communication between Canada and Louisiana. The French constructed forts in western Pennsylvania during 1752 and 1753 even though the British had laid claim to the Ohio Valley years earlier. George Washington was sent by the governor to warn the French that they were trespassing on English land. The French rejected this claim and in the spring of 1745 they built another fort, Fort Duquesne, at the confluence of the Allegheny and Monongahela Rivers, at the present site of Pittsburgh, where the Ohio River originates. Washington led a relatively small band of Virginia *militiamen* against a force of approximately 500 French soldiers and 400 Native Americans. Outnumbered, Washington ultimately surrendered in July 1754. This marked the unofficial start of the French and Indian War. Two years later the fighting spread to Europe, where England and Prussia fought France, Spain, Austria, and Russia from 1756 to 1763 in what became known as the Seven Years' War (Reich 270).

A costly war by all accounts, this major event in American history ended with the signing of the Peace of Paris in 1763. This treaty resulted in France *relinquishing* Canada and all land east of the Mississippi River to England. France turned over several Caribbean islands to England. Spain surrendered Florida to retain islands in the gulf of the St. Lawrence River.

In his chronicle *The American Revolution*, Gordon Wood noted,

In 1763, Great Britain straddled the world with the greatest and richest empire since the fall of Rome. From India to the Mississippi River its armies and navies had been victorious. (4)

The Results of the War

The signing of the Peace of Paris in 1763 gave all the lands between the Atlantic Ocean and the Mississippi River to Britain. It did not bring peace to the American frontier (Polk 219), however, for the Native Americans were still a *formidable* force with whom the British had to reckon.

The Road to Revolution

Admittedly, their strength had declined between sickness and the ravages of war, yet those Native Americans living north of the Ohio River were still militarily significant (Polk 219), and if *alliances* among any of the major tribes were allowed to develop, the colonists' future would again be in jeopardy. The British were acutely aware of this potential threat and in an effort to put an end to it, they inadvertently created a backlash that marked the beginning of colonial disagreement, disobedience, and great discord with the mother country.

The Seven Years' War left Britain with a large debt and new financial obligations. The perpetual concern of a Native American attack translated to Britain's acknowledgment that government troops needed to remain in America. However, recognizing that keeping an active military in the colonies was an expensive proposition, the British decided to take action on two fronts. These two actions would "set in motion a chain of events that would ultimately shatter the British Empire" (Wood 5).

A Royal Proclamation

In an effort to *pacify* the Native American population, the British government issued a royal *proclamation* that drew a line north to south through the crest of the Appalachian mountains and forbade settlers to cross that line. And, from the colonists' perspective, to add insult to injury, the British ordered squatters off this land, admitting through this *proclamation* that "great frauds and abuses" had been inflicted upon the Indians (Polk 219). The colonists were incensed by this *proclamation* and viewed Britain's actions as an affront to the colonists' labor, courage, and financial investment in America. After the French and Indian War the colonists felt a sense of relief, a sense of renewal and pride, as well as a sense of adventure regarding prospective lands to the west. The *edict* was flatly ignored not just by the settlers and homesteaders but by merchants, plantation owners, and members of assemblies (Polk 221).

Taxation

The second action taken by the British that angered the colonists was the passage of a series of acts whose primary purpose was to generate *revenue* to help pay for the British army in America. First came the Sugar Act, in 1764, which forced colonists to pay taxes on sugar, coffee, wine, dye, and other goods. Then the Stamp Act of 1765 declared that legal documents, newspapers, pamphlets, and items such as dice and playing cards must have stamps affixed to them. Though the Sugar Act did not sit well with the colonists, the Stamp Act outraged them. Colonial opposition groups began to form, with some adopting the name "Sons of Liberty." Outbreaks of violence began to occur in Boston and other parts of New England, and petitions were drafted and signed urging King George to repeal the Stamp Act.

From the British *perspective*, these taxes were needed. By taxing the colonists, Parliament was able to reduce taxes in Britain while generating much-needed revenue to support the British army in America. The mindset in Britain was that the colonists needed to contribute to the years of protection that the British government had provided. To further emphasize this point, Parliament passed the *Quartering* Act in 1765, which required colonists to house and feed British soldiers.

As a result of incessant demonstrations and harassment of tax collectors and stamp distributors, Parliament repealed the Stamp Act in 1766. However, led by the king's new minister of finance, Charles Townsend, Parliament passed an even heftier series of taxes on paper, lead, glass, paint, and tea. These acts, known as the Townsend Acts, triggered even greater dissent among the colonists, with many protest meetings as well as a series of newspaper essays, all urging colonists to resist British *oppression*. In 1767, John Dickinson's "Letters from a Farmer in Pennsylvania to Inhabitants of the British Colonies," argued that the Townsend Acts "trampled upon colonial rights" (*American Revolution Almanac*, Bigelow and Schmittroth xvi). Dickinson was actually a mild-mannered lawyer with strong Quaker roots, and therefore a *pacifist* at heart.

The British logic in exercising the Townsend Acts was that, since the colonists could not, or would not, accept the direct, or internal taxation as reflected in the stamp tax, then the government would have to gather revenue through indirect or external customs duties (Wood 31). Dickinson felt that the duties were as unjust as taxes. Yet he *advocated* a non-violent response to the British legislation. In his essays, Dickinson suggested that the colonists boycott those British goods that fell under the Townsend Acts.

Dickinson's essays, about a dozen in all, first appeared in newspapers, but were later reproduced in pamphlet form. Pamphlets had become a popular means of communicating at the time. Dickinson's writings were read widely, both in England and America, with many Americans feeling his position on the issue of taxation and duties reflected theirs perfectly. According to Bigelow and Schmittroth, "his argument would turn up again and again in the many writings and speeches that appeared before the war for independence actually broke out" (54).

The colonists' *boycott* of British goods was successful, with British exports to America showing a dramatic decrease. In 1770 the Townsend Acts were finally repealed, and duties were lifted from all but one *commodity*, tea.

Conflicts and Confrontations

Tensions grew as colonists were in no way accepting of this tax on tea. Colonists were also growing more and more agitated by the presence of British soldiers, who under the provisions of the Quartering Act were being housed and fed at the colonists' expense. Finally, in 1768, King George sent two *regiments* of troops to Boston to support government officials who were dealing with increased harassment by the locals on a daily basis. Bostonians again felt this show of force was unnecessary, feeling it an insult that their government would have to resort to policing its own citizens at gunpoint. Numerous scuffles and skirmishes played out for several years until finally, in 1770, an exchange of insults between citizens and soldiers escalated to a riotous physical confrontation, with the British soldiers pelted by stones and snowballs. Reinforcements were summoned by the British, and shortly thereafter shots were fired, resulting in the death of five colonists, with six more wounded. This incident became known as the Boston Massacre.

A period of relative calm followed the Boston Massacre. Many felt that the actions of both sides had gotten out of hand. The British even withdrew troops from the western frontier, those being the troops that were deployed to keep the colonists from spilling over into the Native American territory. The peace would not last long, however, as repeated petitioning by the colonists to remove the tea tax went unheeded. Among those petitioning was Benjamin Franklin, who at the time served as a respected colonial agent in England. In 1773, the Tea Act, a new piece of legislation, would instigate colonial dissention and unrest again.

The problem stemmed from the colonists' successful boycott of British tea. As 18 million pounds of East India Company tea sat in a London warehouse, American merchants smuggled in tea from other countries. In an effort to save the East India Company from financial ruin, the British Parliament placed a small tax on East India Company tea but permitted the tea to be shipped directly to American tea agents, drastically reducing its price. Even with the imposed tax, the East India tea could then be sold at a cheaper price than any other tea sold by American merchants (65).

The colonists flatly rejected this manipulation by the British, citing this act as another policy of "taxation without representation." In major American port cities, the tea sat and rotted in warehouses; some local officials refused to allow the tea to be unloaded, sending the trading ships back to England with the "poisoned" East India tea, as the taxed tea was referred to by the colonists. This occurred in all but one major port city, that being Boston. In Boston, the governor, loyal to the king, allowed the tea-laden ships to dock, insisting that the taxes would be paid and the tea thereby unloaded. One night, after weeks of sitting in the harbor, the ships were stealthily boarded by *rebel* townsmen who had disguised themselves as Indians. The *rebels*, with small hatchets and clubs in hand, emptied 342 chests of tea into Boston Harbor.

The Boston Tea Party resulted in major *sanctions* inflicted upon the city of Boston. Parliament closed the port of Boston, throwing hundreds of Bostonians out of work. Parliament restructured Massachusetts' government to give the king greater control, and as a final blow, Massachusetts was placed under military rule. These punishing acts were referred to by the British as the *Coercive* Acts of 1774. They were referred to by American colonists as the *Intolerable* Acts of 1774. Soon after the passage of these acts, rioting broke out in the streets of Boston, and later that year the First Continental Congress met in Philadelphia and approved the Declaration and Resolves, which stated that colonists would stop buying British goods until their complaints were heard and issues were resolved. The document also included a declaration of the rights of the colonies. King George III rejected this appeal, believing that the colonies needed to be punished for their rebellious actions.

The Battle of Lexington and Concord

In April 1775, just months after the meeting of the Continental Congress, British troops were sent to Concord to *seize* the small store of weapons that the patriots had begun to gather. En route to Concord, at Lexington, the first *regiment* of redcoats (about 350) encountered a group of 50–75 local *militiamen*, known as *minutemen*. Realizing that they were greatly outnumbered, the *minutemen* began to disperse. At this point accounts vary, but ultimately shots rang out and eight Americans were killed and one British soldier was wounded. Each side claimed the other fired first.

The British sent for reinforcements, as did the *minutemen*. By the next morning 450 Americans faced 700 British soldiers at Concord. The British began to retreat, but were met with even more resistance as they attempted to return to Boston. When all was said and done, 49 Americans lay dead and more than 40 were wounded. The British lost 73 men with 173 wounded, while 28 went missing.

The Imminence of War

The Second Continental Congress met in Philadelphia weeks after the Battle of Lexington and Concord, and George Washington was appointed head of the ragtag army based in Cambridge. Meanwhile, in *retaliation* for the British march on Lexington and Concord, Ethan Allen and his Green Mountain Boys seized Fort Ticonderoga in New York. Congress was surprised to learn of the development and passed a resolution stating that material sized in the takeover of Fort Ticonderoga would be held in storage until Britain and the colonies settled their differences; until the very end, the colonists were hanging on to every hope that a resolution could be achieved.

But King George refused to acknowledge any petition from the Continental Congress. He believed that all of their written communications, no matter how *diplomatically* they had been stated, were merely a charade, and that the colonies were obsessed with the idea of establishing themselves as an independent nation.

Common Sense

In early 1776, Thomas Paine, an Englishman who had arrived in the colonies only two years earlier, seemed to capture the sentiment of Americans in his pamphlet entitled *Common Sense*. Paine, who had been trained as a corsetmaker, had little formal education, but in simple language, he was able to express the "accumulated American rage against George III" (Wood 55). Paine pointed out that the crux of the problem was not the British ministers, nor the Parliament, nor George III, for that matter. The problem, according to Thomas Paine, was *England's constitution*. Paine explained that the British system of government had "two deadly flaws—monarchy and hereditary rule." He stated further that only by governing themselves could Americans secure their freedom and achieve the peace that they had been striving for. As Gordon Wood states, "*Common Sense* was the most *incendiary* and popular pamphlet of the entire Revolutionary era; it went through twenty-five editions in 1776 alone" (55).

The Declaration of Independence

At the end of 1775, King George proclaimed that America was in a state of *rebellion*. Britain placed an *embargo* on American trade and ordered the capture of all American ships. Shortly thereafter it was learned that George III had intentions to hire German *mercenaries* to help squelch the rebellion. These actions by the British, paired with Thomas Paine's *Common Sense*, led the Americans to declare their independence.

The Continental Congress met on June 11, 1776, and elected the Committee of Five—Thomas Jefferson, John Adams, Benjamin Franklin, Roger Sherman, and Robert Livingston. The committee was charged with the task of drafting the public statement that would present to the world the colonies' case for independence. This document was called the Declaration of Independence. Thomas Jefferson, who was noted for the eloquence of his writing, was chosen to draft the document. On July 2, 1776, with only a few minor changes made by the committee, the declaration was presented to Congress. The document stated the three main reasons as to why the colonies must separate from England, those being taxation without representation, the presence of British troops in the colonies, and the trade restrictions imposed on the colonies by King George and the British Parliament. The document also proclaimed that the 13 separate colonies now considered themselves to be one independent, united nation.

On July 9, 1776, the Declaration of Independence was read at Bowling Green in Manhattan. The crowd became so aroused with enthusiasm that they toppled the lead statue of King George III. It has been said that the statue was taken to Connecticut, where it was melted down and turned into 42,000 bullets for American soldiers (Bigelow and Schmittroth 133).

Along with these public announcements for the benefit of the colonists, the Declaration of Independence was, of course, made known around the world. This announcement to the global community was more than just a public notice: it was sending a message to potential *allies* that this was not a civil war; rather it was a war between two independent nations. By declaring the colonies "an independent and united nation," countries such as "France and Spain—Great Britain's longtime enemies—could freely offer their assistance to the United States of America" (Bigelow and Schmittroth 133).

THE REVOLUTIONARY WAR

Great Britain was now reckoning with the fact that what in its eyes had started as an irritating colonial resistance to government authority had, over 13 years, mushroomed into a full-blown war for independence. This war had the potential to exacerbate Great Britain's longstanding struggle with France for global supremacy (Wood 75)

While the Continental Congress was meeting in Philadelphia, the British general William Howe led three ships and 4,000 men to the peninsula of Sandy Hook at the mouth of lower New York Bay. Shortly thereafter he was joined by his brother, Admiral Richard Howe, who came from England with more ships and thousands of Hessians. On July 2, 1776, the day the Declaration of Independence went before Congress for approval, General Howe landed his troops on Staten Island in New York harbor. Howe's ships met no opposition from the Americans (Bigelow and Schmittroth 136).

The Howe brothers did not attack, as was expected; instead, they issued a letter to George Washington, the gist of which was that the British were willing to *pardon* the *rebel* colonists if they would surrender without a fight. Of course, Washington rejected this offer, replying that "those who had committed no fault needed no pardon" (137). Additional British troops and warships arrived in New York, and by August 12, 1776, General Howe had 33,000 soldiers under his command. His brother led 10 large warships, 20 frigates, and 10,000 seamen into the harbor. The Americans were outnumbered two to one.

The colonial army was no match for the British and Hessian troops. Though the fighting dragged on for several weeks, on September 20, 1776, Washington and his men were forced to abandon Manhattan. A few weeks later, the Americans lost a battle on Lake Champlain, on the New York–Vermont border, where again the Americans were ill equipped to compete with the British army. Following the loss at Lake Champlain was another loss in late October at White Plains, New York.

Washington stationed troops in New York and New Jersey while he retreated westward, further into New Jersey, with the main body of his army. This splitting of the American troops proved disastrous, as 2,800 Americans were taken prisoner by the British when they made their last stand to defend Manhattan. This pattern continued, with the British capturing Fort Lee in New Jersey in November. By December 1776, Washington and his ragtag army crossed the Delaware River into Pennsylvania with Cornwallis in hot pursuit. Of the 20,000 men he had started with, Washington had only 2,000 remaining. Many had been killed, but even more had deserted as loss after humiliating loss demoralized the *rebels*. Washington feared the end was near.

Yet on December 13, General Howe made an unexpected announcement. He announced that he was done "making war" for the winter season. This was not an uncommon practice for professional soldiers of the era. However, according to military historian T. Harry Williams in *The History of American Wars from Colonial Times to 1918*, if Howe had moved on to Philadelphia rather than waiting until the spring of 1777, "he undoubtedly could have taken Philadelphia, the largest city in America at the time, and, as the seat of Congress, the capital. He might also have taken the little American army or at least would have destroyed the *rebel* will to continue the war. He was satisfied, however, with what he had accomplished" (61).

Later in the month of December, Washington made a desperate move. Feeling the need to convince the American people and his own troops that all was not lost, he planned a surprise attack on Hessian troops stationed for the winter in Trenton, New Jersey. With reinforcements joining his band, Washington was able to march on to Trenton with an army of 2,400 men. They staged a surprise attack on Christmas Day, overtaking the startled Hessian soldiers, who had been sleeping off their holiday revelry. With additional troops, Washington was able to follow this victory with another in Princeton, just one week later, on January 3, 1777. As a result, all British forts in central New Jersey were abandoned.

Though the morale of the *rebel* army had been restored, Washington sent word to Congress in March 1777 that he was down to 3,000 troops, many of whom were sick with smallpox and all of whom were malnourished. He convinced Congress to offer respectable pay and the promise of land to those who were willing to sign up for service to the Continental Army.

A major turning point in the war occurred in October 1777, when the British general Burgoyne surrendered at Saratoga, New York. Burgoyne was defeated as local *militiamen* teamed with the Continental Army, creating a *formidable* force of 17,000 men that surrounded Burgoyne's army of 7,000. This victory at Saratoga, though not spectacular, convinced the French to throw their support behind the Americans. In December 1777, as Washington and his troops were weathering a brutal winter at Valley Forge, King Louis of France agreed to recognize American independence, thereby providing both monetary and military support to the Americans.

Still seeking revenge stemming from their defeat in the Seven Years' War, the French led the way, with Spain and Holland soon providing financial as well as naval support. By June 1778, the first French naval *fleet* had arrived off the coast of Virginia. General Henry Clinton, fearful that the French would cut him off from British headquarters in New York, abandoned Philadelphia and headed to New York.

In December 1778, Savannah, Georgia, fell to the British, with the rebel army, assisted by the French navy, attempting to retake the city in the fall of 1779. This attempt was unsuccessful, and a blow to the morale of the Americans. Adding to the weakening of the American spirit were the rebel nation's financial woes. At this point, with the fighting having dragged on for almost five years, American *coffers* were running dry. Yet the Americans were not alone. The British had come under attack in the Caribbean. It seemed that the French, recognizing Great Britain's preoccupation with the war in America, felt the opportunity ripe for possibly regaining some of the precious islands in the Caribbean, possessions the French had lost to the British earlier as part of the Peace of Paris treaty. This attack put an additional strain on all British resources. Meanwhile, Benjamin Franklin, having developed outstanding diplomatic relations with France, repeatedly requested loans from the French and was never refused. In the end, French loans, French soldiers, and in great part the French navy were crucial to the Americans' eventual success.

After Burgoyne's surrender at Saratoga, the British shifted their attention to the South, with Savannah as their first target. Savannah became the British center for southern operations. In February 1780, soon after the fall of Savannah, Charleston came under attack, and though the patriots resisted incessant brutal attacks (the siege lasted three months), it too fell to the British. Another loss at Camden, South Carolina, further deflated the morale of the rebel fighters. However, later that year a victory at King's Mountain, South Carolina, buoyed spirits, and American commanders forced General Charles Cornwallis to leave the Carolinas and retreat to Virginia.

Up to this point, one of the key strategic points of the Revolutionary War had been the fact that the British controlled the American coastal waters. As noted in *The Making of America—Life, Liberty, and the Pursuit of a Nation*,

> *When George Washington wanted to move his troops, they had to walk, whereas the British army could quickly and easily sail anywhere from Boston to Savannah. Even after France sent an army of 6,000 men, under the command of General Jean-Baptiste Rochambeau, to help the Continental cause in 1780, it mattered little. Without a fleet, many of the Continental troops were stranded in the North for almost a year, during which time the focus of the war shifted far away, to the South. (68)*

However, in the spring of 1781, the Marquis de Lafayette convinced King Louis XVI to send a *fleet* to "tip the scales against the British" (*Making of America* 68). With 4,000 troops, the French sailed into Chesapeake Bay on August 5, 1781, surprising the British navy. Meanwhile, Cornwallis was marching his troops through Virginia toward the coast, where he intended to join the British vessels at Yorktown. With the French *fleet* in control of the coastline and Washington and Rochambeau marching toward Virginia from the north, Cornwallis soon found his armies trapped on the Yorktown Peninsula. The combined American and French troops totaled more than 16,000, while Cornwallis had less than half that number. Yet the battle raged on for 10 weeks, with the British general hoping against hope for relief by the British troops stationed in New York. That help never came, and on October 19, 1781, Cornwallis was forced to surrender. This marked the end of the Revolutionary War. Two years later, the Treaty of Paris was signed, with the British recognizing independence and *ceding* all the territory between the Atlantic and the Mississippi, south of Canada and north of the Gulf of Mexico (except New Orleans and Spain's colony in Florida), to the new United States of America.

Keywords and Terms

1. advocated
2. alliances
3. allies
4. boycott
5. ceding
6. coercive
7. coffers
8. commodity

9. diplomatically
10. edict
11. embargo
12. fleet
13. formidable
14. incendiary
15. intolerable
16. mercenaries
17. militiamen
18. minutemen
19. oppression
20. pacifist
21. pacify
22. pardon
23. perspective
24. proclamation
25. quartering
26. rebellion
27. rebels
28. regiment
29. regiments
30. relinquishing
31. retaliation
32. revenue
33. sanctions
34. seize
35. skirmishes
36. squatter

BIBLIOGRAPHY

Begelow, B., and L. Schmittroth. *American Revolution: Almanac*. Detroit, MI: UXL–Gale Group, 2000.

Hakim, Joy. *A History of US, Book Three, From Colonies to Country*. New York: Oxford University Press, 2003.

The Making of America—Life, Liberty, and the Pursuit of a Nation. New York: TIME, 2005.

Polk, W.R. *The Birth of America, from before Columbus to the Revolution*. New York: HarperCollins, 2008.

Quigley, C., and K. Rodriguez. *We the People: The Citizens and the Constitution.* Calabasas, CA: Center for Civic Education, 2007.

Reich, Jerome. *Colonial America* (5th ed.). Upper Saddle River, NJ: Prentice Hall, 2001.

Williams, Harry. *The History of American Wars from Colonial Times to 1918.* New York: Alfred A. Knopf, 1981.

Wood, Gordon S. *The American Revolution: A History.* New York: Random House, 2002.

11

The American Revolution: Book 1

Title: *The Year of the Hangman*
Author: Gary Blackwood
Grade/Age: Ages 14 and up
ISBN: 9780142400784
NCSS Standards: 1,2,3,4,5,6,8

ANNOTATION

Set during the American Revolution, this book takes readers on a "what if" journey. What if the Americans had lost the Revolutionary War? Readers follow the main character, 15-year-old Creighton, as he is kidnapped and sent to live with his uncle. Unexpectedly, he finds himself living and working for Dr. Benjamin Franklin. He struggles with the idea of what side he is on as he goes from young boy to young man.

SUGGESTED VOCABULARY

abysmal, American Revolution, antagonize, apprentice, assailants, bayou, bluffing, brigands, civilians, clergymen, cloak, commiserate, constable, countrymen, crapulence, cutlass, dinghy, dumbfounded, epithet, execution, fortnight, gauche, gentry, gout, handbills, highwaymen, impermanence, incredulously, ingratiate, invective, knaves, mastiff, merchants, militia, minuets, nonchalant, oakum, palisade, pence, pension, petulantly, pirates, precarious, precipitously, privateers, propaganda, quadrille, quibble, ruffians, shillings, shrewdness, smallpox, squander, supercilious, tinderbox, traitors, uchronia, warmongers, wastrels

BEFORE READING: PREPARING TO JUMP INTO THE BOOK

Playing Hangman

Play a game of hangman with students using a vocabulary word from the vocabulary terms listed in the previous section. Then, ask students to theorize how the game of hangman originated. Next, allow students to use the internet to research the origins of the game. Students write five facts they learn about the history of the game and share with the class. To conclude, distribute the Vocabulary List in Figure 11.1 and allow students to play a few rounds of hangman. Ask students if they view the spelling game differently now. Require students to define the words at the conclusion of the hangman games.

Vocabulary List

1. abysmal
2. American Revolution
3. antagonize
4. apprentice
5. assailants
6. bayou
7. bluffing
8. brigands
9. civilians
10. clergymen
11. cloak
12. commiserate
13. constable
14. countrymen
15. crapulence
16. cutlass
17. dinghy
18. dumbfounded
19. epithet
20. execution
21. fortnight
22. gauche
23. gentry
24. gout
25. handbills
26. highwaymen
27. impermanence
28. incredulously
29. ingratiate
30. invective
31. knaves
32. mastiff
33. merchants
34. militia
35. minuets
36. nonchalant
37. oakum
38. palisade
39. pence
40. pension
41. petulantly
42. pirates
43. precarious
44. precipitously
45. privateers
46. propaganda
47. quadrille
48. quibble
49. ruffians
50. shillings
51. shrewdness
52. smallpox
53. squander
54. supercilious
55. tinderbox
56. traitors
57. uchronia
58. warmongers
59. wastrels

Figure 11.1: Vocabulary List

From *Beyond the Textbook: Using Trade Books and Databases to Teach Our Nation's History, Grades 7–12* by Carianne Bernadowski, Robert Del Greco, and Patricia L. Kolencik. Santa Barbara, CA: Libraries Unlimited. Copyright © 2013.

Paul Revere: Using the PIC Strategy

Students will read two documents and analyze the information in order to make predictions about the text. The first text students will read *Paul Revere: Account of His Midnight Ride to Concord and Lexington (1775)*, which can be found online or in the school library's history database. The second text students will read is *The Landlord's Tale: Paul Revere's Ride*, found at <http://www.paulreveresride.org/>.

Before reading each text, classroom teachers and/or school librarians distribute the PIC Handout found in Figure 11.2. Students should consider the following:

1. What is the **P**urpose of the reading?
2. What are the **I**mportant ideas?
3. What **C**onnections can they make?

After reading, students should complete the "after reading" column where they are asked to respond to the same questions after reading. Finally, students should create three questions for each text they are still unsure about and use the questions to guide their reading.

What If?

Ask students to engage in a class discussion on the theme of "What if America had not won the American Revolutionary War?" Allow students to make a class list of what might be different both in history and today.

Colonies

Students create a colonial timeline using a primary source from which to gather information. Students can create a handmade or electronic timeline. Students can make an electronic timeline at <http://www.free-timeline.com/timeline.jsp>. Classroom teachers or school librarians can display the timelines in the classroom or library.

Discovering Alternate History

Explain to students that *The Year of the Hangman* is alternative history; that is, history that asks the reader to think in terms of "what if" while reading. Show students the website <http://uchronia.net/intro.html> and explain that this book is crafted in such a way as to make the reader think deeply about the "what ifs" while reading. Students should read critically and determine whether historical fact or author liberty is present in the text.

DURING READING: GUIDED DISCUSSION QUESTIONS

1. At the opening of Chapter 1, Creighton's mother says "a bad end." What is she implying?
2. Why was 1777 called the "year of the hangman"?
3. Why do you think Creighton enjoys witnessing executions?
4. How does Creighton view school? What does he enjoy doing instead of attending school? Describe some of the mischief for which he is involved.
5. What is your first impression of Creighton?
6. Explain the difference between a gentleman and a merchant.
7. Describe the exchange between Creighton and Thomas that occurs on page 9.

PIC Handout

Text One

Before Reading	After Reading	Questions
What is the **P**urpose of the reading?	What was the **P**urpose of the reading?	#1
What are the **I**mportant ideas?	What were the **I**mportant ideas?	#2
What **C**onnections can you make?	What **C**onnections can you now make?	#3

Text Two

Before Reading	After Reading	Questions
What is the **P**urpose of the reading?	What was the **P**urpose of the reading?	#1
What are the **I**mportant ideas?	What were the **I**mportant ideas?	#2
What **C**onnections can you make?	What **C**onnections can you now make?	#3

Figure 11.2: PIC Handout

From *Beyond the Textbook: Using Trade Books and Databases to Teach Our Nation's History, Grades 7–12* by Carianne Bernadowski, Robert Del Greco, and Patricia L. Kolencik. Santa Barbara, CA: Libraries Unlimited. Copyright © 2013.

8. What happens at the card game on page 12?
9. Describe Creighton's kidnappers. Who do you think they might be?
10. Why do you think Creighton's captors take him on board a ship? Where do you think they might be taking him?
11. What would be your reaction to Creighton's mother's letter on page 24?
12. Describe the exchange between Hale and Creighton aboard the ship.
13. What do Creighton and Hale have in common?
14. Why does Creighton's mother send him away? What does he plan to do? What would you do?
15. Describe the Colonel, Creighton's uncle. Why is his face scarred?
16. Why do the men leave Charles Town?
17. What does Creighton think of Florida?
18. How does the Florida of 1777 differ from the Florida of today?
19. What is Creighton's plan once they arrive in Florida? Does he follow through with his plan? Why or why not?
20. Describe the attack on the *Amity*.
21. Who is Benedict Arnold? Describe him in detail.
22. What is a bound servant? Why does Creighton pretend to be a bound servant?
23. What do the Americans do with the dead on board the ship? Do you think this is fact or fiction? Why or why not?
24. Why are the British soldiers afraid to go to New Orleans?
25. Why do you think Hale will not renounce his loyalty to the king?
26. What information do you think Creighton's uncle has about his father?
27. Describe New Orleans as presented in the book.
28. Why is Creighton surprised to meet Dr. Franklin?
29. Why does Franklin's maid get angry at the end of Chapter 6?
30. What happens when Ben Franklin and Creighton play cards? What is the outcome?
31. Why do you think Franklin uses Creighton as a proofreader?
32. What does Creighton learn about Franklin and his newspaper? What do you predict he will do with that information?
33. What happens to Jefferson's family?
34. Why does Franklin leave Philadelphia? Would you have done the same? Why or why not?
35. Describe what Creighton believes to be rebel propaganda.
36. Why does Creighton begin to feel guilty about reading Franklin's secret messages?
37. How does Creighton get a pistol for his uncle?
38. Describe how Creighton begins to change his loyalties. Cite examples from the text.
39. Describe what happens when Creighton visits his uncle at the jail.
40. Who does Creighton meet playing cards?
41. What happened to Creighton's father? How does Creighton react when he learns this information?
42. Why do you think the bandits lit Franklin's printing shop on fire?
43. How does Franklin die? Is this historically accurate?
44. How does Sophie react to Franklin's death? Why do you think the reacts in this manner? What does he plan to do? What does Creighton plan to do?

45. General Arnold has a plan on page 186–187. Explain his plan.
46. How is Creighton like his father? Explain.
47. How does Creighton betray the Englishman in Chapter 19? How did this make you feel?
48. Why does Gowers go through with the duel?
49. How does Creighton react to his uncle's death? Is this how you expected him to react? Why or why not?
50. Who is held in cell number four in the jail? Is that who you expected?
51. Describe the rescue of Harry Brown. How did this make you feel?
52. What was your reaction to the ending of the story?

AFTER READING: CONNECTING TO THE TEXT

Tracking Translation

Ask students to revisit the text and find French words and their English translations. Students can use the Tracking Translation handout in Figure 11.3. The classroom teacher or school librarian can use the words as a word wall or for additional study of the French language.

Scene Comic Strip

Allow students to work in partners or small groups to create a comic strip based on a scene from the book. Students should create a rough draft using plan white paper and pencil. Require students to include a distinct setting as well as characters and dialogue. The scene that is being portrayed should be clear to readers. The classroom teacher and/or school librarian should collect and copy all comics and bind them into a class book for class distribution or placement in the school library. The Scene Comic Strip Rubric found in Figure 11.4 can be used for assessment purposes.

Creating a Time Capsule

Students work in small groups to collect information and/or pictures of artifacts that could be included in a time capsule for the American Revolution. Students write a brief explanation of the role that each item plays. Time capsule items should be shared with the entire class.

Vocabulary Miming

Distribute the vocabulary words to students and allow them to act them out without words. The remainder of the class has to guess the word.

DIGGING INTO THE DATABASE

Examining Documents

Students use the school library's history database to examine various documents from the American Revolution. Students can choose a poster, quote, map, or political cartoon to read, analyze, and share with the group. Students should be able to explain the relevance to the text and the American Revolution.

Tracking Translations

French Word	English Translation

Figure 11.3: Tracking Translations

Scene Comic Strip Rubric

Criteria	4	3	2	1
Characters	Includes all characters, and their relevance to the scene is evident.	Includes all characters, and their relevance to the scene is somewhat evident.	Includes some of the characters, and their relevance to the scene is evident.	Some characters are excluded, and their relevance is not evident.
Setting	The setting of the scene is highly evident.	The setting of the scene is evident.	The setting of the scene is somewhat evident.	The setting of the scene is missing.
Dialogue	The dialogue is related to the characters and is accurate.	The dialogue is somewhat related to the characters and is somewhat accurate.	The dialogue is either unrelated to the characters or is inaccurate.	The dialogue is unrelated to the characters and is inaccurate.
Mechanics	There are no errors in capitalization, punctuation, and/or spelling.	There is one error in capitalization, punctuation, and/or spelling.	There are two errors in capitalization, punctuation, and/or spelling.	There are three or more errors in capitalization, punctuation, and/or spelling.

Figure 11.4: Scene Comic Strip Rubric

From *Beyond the Textbook: Using Trade Books and Databases to Teach Our Nation's History, Grades 7–12* by Carianne Bernadowski, Robert Del Greco, and Patricia L. Kolencik. Santa Barbara, CA: Libraries Unlimited. Copyright © 2013.

Soldier Poster

Students use the history database to examine the types of propaganda used to recruit soldiers during the war. Students work in groups to create their own posters for display in the library.

Franklin's Almanac

Students read an excerpt from *Poor Richard's Almanack,* found online or in the school library's history database. The classroom teacher and/or school librarian can conduct a class interpretation and discussion of the writing.

Jay Treaty

Students read about the Jay Treaty using the information found in the school library's database. Using the Question Answer Relationship strategy, students will write two questions per category to ask classmates who have read the same information. Students can work with partners or in small groups to accomplish this task. The goal is to read critically and form questions that will help readers make multiple connections. A blank Question Answer Relationship template can be found in Figure 6.5.

READ ALIKES

Arundel by Kenneth Roberts ISBN 9780892723645 (Young Adult/Adult)

Burr by Gore Vidal ISBN 9780375708732 (Young Adult/Adult)

Drums by James Boyd ISBN 9780766194618 (Young Adult/Adult)

The Fighting Ground by Avi ISBN 9780064401852 (Young Adult/Adult)

Guns for General Washington: A Story of the American Revolution by Seymour Reit ISBN 9780152164355 (Ages 9–12)

The Hessian by Howard Fast ISBN 9781563246012 (Young Adult/Adult)

Oliver Wiswell by Kenneth Roberts ISBN 9781153523332 (Young Adult/Adult)

Rabble in Arms by Kenneth Roberts ISBN 9780892723867 (Young Adult/Adult)

Ruffles and Drums by Betty Cavanna ISBN 9780816712670 (Ages 9–12)

Time Enough for Drums by Ann Rinaldi ISBN 9780440228509 (Young Adult/Adult)

12

The American Revolution: Book 2

Title: *Spy!*
Author: Anna Myers
Grade/Age: Ages 10 and up
ISBN: 9780802797421
NCSS Standards: 1,2,3,4,5,6,8

ANNOTATION

The life of Jonah Hawkins, a young boy, is intertwined with that of Nathan Hale in this historical novel. Jonah promised his dying father that he would remain loyal to the king and never join the patriots in their fight against the king. Master Nathan Hale inspires Jonah to learn and think about the nation's growing turmoil, and his influence might well change Jonah's mind. Eventually Jonah has to decide where his loyalties lie in this unsure time in American history.

SUGGESTED VOCABULARY

admonished, anguish, askew, bayonet, benefactor, beseech, besotted, britches, cat o' nine tails, Coercive Acts, constable, crocus, delegates, forestall, grievances, haughty, haversack, hearth, hornbook, immortality, indignation, Intolerable Acts, jubilant, kinsmen, liquidate, loyalist, mansion, noontide, Parliament, plundering, Rebel, Redcoats, regiment, scoundrel, settee, slough, spectacles, suitors, tankard, treason, undertaker, unfurled, warmonger, zealous

BEFORE READING: PREPARING TO JUMP INTO THE BOOK

Previewing the Book

Nathan Hale said, "I only regret that I have but one life to give for my country." Write the quote on the board and ask students to read the quote and jot down any ideas that come to mind. Ask students, "Why would someone say that? In what circumstances would someone say that?" Next, look at the title and cover of the book and ask students to predict what the book will be about. Write students' predictions on chart paper and hang the list in the classroom or library. While reading the novel, periodically review the predictions and confirm or revise them.

Learning about Nathan Hale

Place students in pairs or small groups to investigate the life of Nathan Hale. Students should take on the following roles as they research: Reader, Scribe, Investigator, and Fact-Finder. Students work in small groups to record and report information about his life. Once students have gathered the information, they elect a reporter to tell the class about what they learn about Nathan Hale in reference to their particular area. The areas of investigation can include: Personality, Childhood, Teaching Career, and Military Service. Each group should include a visual of some type to enhance their information. The following websites could be helpful to students:

<http://www.earlyamerica.com/review/2001_summer_fall/n_hale.html>
<http://www.connecticutsar.org/patriots/hale_nathan.htm>
<http://www.u-s-history.com/pages/h550.html>

Radio Show Performance

Divide class into two groups, or 11 students per group. There are 11 speaking parts in the radio show found at <http://www.readbookonline.net/readOnLine/47627/>. Another option is to allow students to perform two parts each. Classroom teachers or school librarians can print the script found at the above website and explain to students that before television, families would enjoy radio shows; this was a major form of entertainment. Actors on the radio must use only their voices to convey many things to the audience. Provide plenty of time for students to practice. Note: There are 10 characters and one announcer.

Once students feel ready to perform, allow them to do so as you audiotape the performance. Then allow students to listen to their recordings and self-evaluate their performances. Students should listen carefully to their voice intonation, pitch, volume, and expression.

Colonial America

Classroom teachers or school librarians can produce a U.S. map using the mapmaker found at <http://education.nationalgeographic.com/education/mapping/outline-map/?-map=North_America&ar_a=1>. Students then use multiple resources to locate and identify the 13 colonies. You can check students' work with the map at <http://library.thinkquest.org/10966/map.shtml?tqskip1=1>.

DURING READING: GUIDED DISCUSSION QUESTIONS

1. Describe the scene in Chapter 1. What characters do we meet, and in what circumstances do we meet them? Describe their relationship.
2. What is the significance of the date?
3. What does Captain Hale say before he dies? What do you think this means?
4. Jonah screams, "Cut him down." Why do you think screaming this is dangerous?
5. Why does Jonah decide to not return to the inn?
6. Describe how Nathan becomes a teacher.
7. How do Nathan and Samuel differ in their political views? Explain.
8. How does Master Hale help Jonah on page 13?
9. Jonah says he is a "Latin scholar." What does he mean by this? Cite an example from the text.

10. Describe Master Hale's first day of teaching. Is it what you would expect? Why or why not?
11. Describe Betsy Lawrence.
12. Describe the relationship between Nathan and Samuel. Can you relate to this in any way? If so, how?
13. Explain why Samuel visits Nathan's home on page 28.
14. Why do the boys fight in the schoolyard?
15. We learn that Jonah and Mercy's father will die. What do you predict will happen to the children?
16. On his deathbed, Jonah's father says, "Jonah, be careful of the whale." What does this mean?
17. Describe the interaction between Nathan and Betsy at the riverbank.
18. What important possession does the father leave the children (Jonah and Mercy)?
19. What happens to the children after their father's death?
20. How does Jonah feel when the reverend gives him the bill? How would you react?
21. Why does Jonah want to run when he first sees Samuel's mansion?
22. What is the first thing Miss Jayne does for the children upon their arrival?
23. Why is Jonah so happy to see a desk in his new room?
24. How do Jayne and Samuel's views on educating girls differ?
25. At the end of Chapter 6, we learn that Nathan and Betsy's relationship is blooming. What do you predict will happen?
26. Who are the school proprietors?
27. Why do you think Jonah sleeps on the floor his first two nights in the house?
28. What happens when Jonah takes his teacher's book without permission?
29. What kindness does Jonah's teacher show him in Chapter 7? How do you think Jonah felt?
30. Why is Samuel dismissed from the school proprietor board? How does Nathan react?
31. What gift does Mr. Samuel give Jonah at the beginning of Chapter 9? How does he react?
32. How does Jonah save Mr. Samuel's life?
33. Why does Master Hale become a soldier? Do you agree or disagree with his decision? Explain.
34. Nathan meets George Washington. Describe this meeting.
35. Why does Jonah worry so much about Mr. Samuel? Do you think this is necessary? Why or why not?
36. At the end of Chapter 11, the tailor offends Jonah. Describe this exchange.
37. What does the post master rider tell Matthew Green? What is your reaction?
38. We learn the true meaning of the song "Yankee Doodle." Explain. How does this apply to the battles at Concord and Lexington?
39. How does Mercy say goodbye to Nathan?
40. What does Nathan do with his horse before leaving for New York?
41. We learn that the Continental Congress names a general. Who is it?
42. Nathan does not march with the militia as planned. What does he do instead?
43. At the end of Chapter 12, we meet a new Nathan Hale. How has he changed since the beginning of the book?
44. Why do so many American colonists hate Tories? What does that mean?
45. What does Nathan learn when he arrives in New York? Describe his reaction.

46. Compare the New York City in the book to the New York City of today.
47. Nathan and Asher are reunited. Describe this interaction.
48. Why is Nathan's father so angry with Samuel on page 114?
49. Why does General Washington send the army to New York?
50. Why do you think Nathan decides to become a spy for Washington? Would you have done the same? Why or why not?
51. What will be Nathan's cover as a spy? Do you predict he will be successful? Why or why not?
52. How do the children react to Nathan in New York? To Jonah? To Mercy? To Thomas?
53. Why does Jonah tell Samuel about Master Hale? Would you have done the same?
54. What happens to Nathan as he is leaving New York?
55. What are Nathan's last words? Why are these words significant? What do you think his words mean?
56. Why does Jonah return to Artillery Park at the beginning of Chapter 17?
57. Do you think Jonah is justified in being angry with Samuel? Explain.
58. What does Jonah eventually ask of Thomas?
59. Were you surprised by the actions of Jonah and Mercy in the park? Why or why not?
60. How do you feel about the ending of the book? What significance does this play in history?

AFTER READING: CONNECTING TO THE TEXT

Spy Letters

Students investigate and interpret the spy letters found at <http://www2.si.umich.edu/spies/index-gallery.html>. Students then write letters as if they were spies during the American Revolution. Students may find the letter written on June 27, 1779, from George Washington to Benjamin Tallmadge especially interesting. Students' letters should be written from an appropriate place with an accurate date. The letters can be written to people of their choice. Students should write the letter by hand and use language appropriate for that time period in history.

Investigating a Timeline

Classroom teachers and/or school librarians print the timeline found at <http://www.timepage.org/spl/13timeline.html> and distribute it to small groups of students. Students then identify two related activities on the timeline and prepare a presentation of facts for the class.

Reciprocal Teaching

Divide students into small groups with four per group. Distribute the Reciprocal Teaching Guide in Figure 12.1 to define students' jobs in their small groups. Students will be using the Reciprocal Teaching strategy to read and analyze the non-fiction text found at <http://www.leben.us/volume-06-volume-6-issue-2/304-nathan-hale>. Students can write their answers in the Reciprocal Teaching Answer Sheet found in Figure 12.2.

Each student assumes his or her role and acts accordingly. After each group has conducted its reading and its tasks, bring the class together to discuss the article and any additional information students learned about Nathan Hale that they did not learn from the book.

Reciprocal Teaching Guide

Summarizer	Questioner
Interact with group by discussing and documenting important parts of the selection.	Ask questions related to main ideas in the text and be sure to include higher-level questions. Require group members to "read between the lines," or make inferences.
Clarifier	**Predictor**
Help group members make connections between texts and their background knowledge and previous experiences; help them understand confusing parts of the text and unknown vocabulary.	Activate group members' background knowledge by making educated guesses and asking thought-provoking questions; help them by making and revising predictions, and/or confirming these predictions.

Figure 12.1: Reciprocal Teaching Guide

Reciprocal Teaching Answer Sheet

Summarizer	Questioner

Clarifier	Predictor

Figure 12.2: Reciprocal Teaching Answer Sheet

Could You Be a Spy?

Ask students what type of person a spy might be. Make a class list of qualities of a "spy." Then allow students to take the personality quiz on the CIA website at <https://www.cia.gov/careers/cia-personality-quiz.html>. Although this quiz is for fun, lead students in a discussion of what a career in the CIA might entail. How might this be similar to or different from Nathan Hale's mission?

DIGGING INTO THE DATABASE

Dressing the Part

Students use the school library's history database to investigate clothing worn in colonial America. Students then create their interpretations of the clothing either by making actual clothing or by using drawing materials, clay, paint, or other media forms. Display creations in the library or hallway display case.

You Are Invited to a Tea Party!

Each student must visit the school library's history database to learn one important or interesting fact about the Boston Tea Party. Then, the classroom teacher or school librarian plans a tea party where students sit around the table and share their interesting facts. The classroom teacher or school librarian may want to divide the class into smaller groups so the tea parties are not too large in size.

News Story

Students pick one battle from the American Revolution and write a news story for the battle. Students should begin by completing the Newspaper Article Lead worksheet found in Figure 12.3. Once the lead is written students can write the article, including accurate historical dates, names, and other facts. Remind students that straight or hard news stories do not include personal opinions. Classroom teachers or school librarians can use the News Article Rubric in Figure 12.4 for assessment purposes. Once students have completed their articles, bind them with string or spiral binding to allow students to take them home and read them, then place them in a classroom or in the library for circulation.

Cornell Notetaking and Summary Writing

Students read information about the American Revolution either online or in the school library's history database. While students are reading, they use the Cornell Notes Page in Figure 12.5 to take important notes on the reading. Students write the important facts in the left-hand column and notes in the note section. Classroom teachers and school librarians should model this strategy with students prior to requiring students to use it independently. Next, students use their notes to write a succinct summary of the information learned about the American Revolution. The Summary Rubric in Figure 12.6 can be used for assessment purposes.

Newspaper Article Lead

Who? _____

What? _____

When? _____

Where? _____

Why? _____

How? _____ (optional)

Figure 12.3: Newspaper Article Lead

News Article Rubric

	4	3	2	1
Lead	The article has a strong lead that includes the 5 Ws and is written in an extremely effective manner.	The article includes a lead that includes the 5 Ws.	The article includes a lead but does not include all the required elements.	The article does not include a lead.
Supporting Details	Provides a sufficient number of supporting details that relate directly to the lead.	Provides a number of supporting details that relate to the lead.	Provides one or two supporting details that relate to the lead.	Does not provide any supporting details.
Mechanics	The writing has no mechanical errors.	The writing has 1–2 mechanical errors.	The writing has 3–4 mechanical errors.	The writing has 5 or more mechanical errors.
Spelling	The writing has no spelling errors.	The writing has one spelling error.	The writing has two spelling errors.	The writing has three or more spelling errors.

Figure 12.4: News Article Rubric

From *Beyond the Textbook: Using Trade Books and Databases to Teach Our Nation's History, Grades 7–12* by Carianne Bernadowski, Robert Del Greco, and Patricia L. Kolencik. Santa Barbara, CA: Libraries Unlimited. Copyright © 2013

Cornell Notes Page

Important Information	Notes

Figure 12.5: Cornell Notes Page

Summary Rubric

	2	**1**	**0**
Historical Accuracy	Information included in summary is historically accurate.	Summary includes 1–2 inaccuracies in historical information.	Summary includes 3 or more inaccuracies in historical information.
Mechanics	There are 0 errors in capitalization, punctuation, and/or grammar.	There is 1 error in capitalization, punctuation, and/or grammar.	There are more than 2 errors in capitalization, punctuation, and/or grammar.
Summary	Included an appropriate and accurate summary of main idea(s) in 3–4 paragraphs or more.	Includes a somewhat appropriate and accurate summary of main idea(s) in 3–4 paragraphs.	Does not include an appropriate and accurate summary of main idea(s) OR is not 3–4 paragraphs in length.

Figure 12.6: Summary Rubric

From *Beyond the Textbook: Using Trade Books and Databases to Teach Our Nation's History, Grades 7–12* by Carianne Bernadowski, Robert Del Greco, and Patricia L. Kolencik. Santa Barbara, CA: Libraries Unlimited. Copyright © 2013

READ ALIKES

April Morning by Howard Fast ISBN 9780553273229 (Ages 9–12)

The Bloody Country by James Lincoln Collier and Christopher Collier ISBN 9780812438659 (Young Adult/ Adult)

I'm Deborah Sampson: A Soldier of the American Revolution by Patricia Clapp ISBN 9780688417994 (Young Adult/Adult)

John Treegate's Musket by Leonard Wibberley ISBN 9781932350166 (Ages 9–12)

Johnny Tremain by Esther Forbes ISBN 9780547614328 (Ages 9–12)

Liberty or Death: The American Revolution: 1763–1783 by Betsy Maestro ISBN 9780688088026 (Ages 9–12)

My Brother Sam Is Dead by James Lincoln Collier and Christopher Collier ISBN 9780439783606 (Young Adult/Adult)

Peter Treegate's War by Leonard Wibberley ISBN 9781932350210 (Young Adult/Adult)

The Reb and the Redcoats by Constance Savery ISBN 9781883937423 (Young Adult/Adult)

The Winter Hero by James Lincoln Collier and Christopher Collier ISBN 9780590426046 (Young Adult/Adult)

13

Acquisition of New Lands— The Louisiana Purchase: An Introduction to Teaching This Time Period

In the companion volume to the PBS documentary of the same name, *Lewis and Clark: The Journey of the Corps of Discovery* (1997), Duncan and Burns share that when Thomas Jefferson became President in 1801, two out of every three Americans lived within 50 miles of the Atlantic Ocean, with only four roads crossing the Allegheny Mountains. At that time, the United States ended on the eastern banks of the Mississippi River and most of the west was still a great unknown to those living on the eastern side of the continent (5). Though the Spanish, with their interests in the southwest, had explored and attempted to settle in parts of Texas and California, and the English, with their focus on fur trade to the north, had established settlements and trading posts in Canada, it was the French who were holding the vast territory stretching from the Mississippi River to the Rocky Mountains. This territory, called Louisiana, stretched across the heart of the North American continent.

Joining France, Spain, England, and even Russia (which had outposts in Alaska and had built a fort on the northern coast of California) in their interest in the resource-rich land was, of course, the young United States of America. President Jefferson was fascinated by the mystery, and the potential, of the west. Also, much like the others, Jefferson believed in the existence of the Northwest Passage. He believed that a river, or a series of rivers, must exist and, connected together, crossed the western mountains, reaching the Pacific coast, thereby facilitating trade with the Orient. Jefferson believed that whichever nation discovered the Northwest Passage and gained control of it would "control the destiny of the continent" (Duncan and Burns 7).

Thomas Jefferson was considered by many to be an expansionist president, possessing a vision for a United States that stretched all the way to the Pacific coast. By the time of his election, the Mississippi and Ohio River valleys had been flooded by hundreds of thousands of American farmers searching for fertile land. These farmers relied upon the Mississippi river to transport their harvested crops down to New Orleans to either sell at markets or to export abroad. President Jefferson realized that maintaining control of this strategic port was critical to the economic well-being of the United States. As Jefferson himself put it, whoever controlled this port had "a hand on the throat of the American economy" (Ambrose 12).

President Jefferson envisioned a United States that would extend to the Pacific coast in an "Empire of Liberty" (Ambrose 11). The purchase of the Louisiana Territory from France in 1803 represented a major step toward the fulfillment of that vision. In 1803, and for a price of only $15 million (about 3 cents an acre), the newly formed United States was able to increase its landmass by approximately 828,000 square miles. This nearly doubled the size of the young nation. Out of this vast territory came all of Arkansas, Missouri, Iowa, Oklahoma, Kansas, and Nebraska, and parts of Minnesota, North Dakota, South Dakota, New Mexico, Texas, Montana, Wyoming, Colorado, and, of course, Louisiana.

In order to gain a proper perspective on the significance of the Louisiana Purchase, it is important to examine the unique circumstances that allowed for the purchase of the Louisiana Territory from France in 1803. Several factors contributed to both the United States' desire to acquire the expansive territory and France's willingness to part with it at a seemingly discounted price. Also, it is necessary to discuss the extraordinary journey of Lewis and Clark. Following the Louisiana Purchase, Meriwether Lewis and William Clark were tasked by President Jefferson with leading an expedition to explore the vast wilderness of the west. They were able to gather huge amounts of valuable information about the area's landscapes, climates, plants, animals, and resources, as well as about the people inhabiting this largely unknown land.

HISTORICAL CONTEXT AND MOTIVATING FACTORS

France had claimed the land comprising the Louisiana Territory since the mid-15th century. However, as a result of the French and Indian War, France had *ceded* the Louisiana Territory to Spain in 1762. In 1800, however, Napoleon Bonaparte quietly reacquired the Louisiana Territory from Spain with the intention of rebuilding a French empire in the New World. President Jefferson commented that if the rumors of France's acquisition of the Louisiana Territory were true, "it would be impossible that France and the United States can continue long as friends" (Ambrose 12). Both anxious to avoid war with France and determined to control the Mississippi River, Jefferson sent his close friend, the U.S. minister to France Robert Livingston, as well as Secretary of State James Monroe to France to try to purchase New Orleans.

Jefferson's belief in the importance of maintaining control of New Orleans is evidenced by this excerpt of a letter he wrote to Livingston in April 1802:

> *There is on the globe one single spot, the possessor of which is our natural and habitual enemy. It is New Orleans, through which the produce of three-eighths of our territory must pass to market, and from its fertility it will ere long yield more than half of our whole produce and contain more than half of our inhabitants. France, placing herself in that door, assumes to us the attitude of defiance. . . . The day that France takes possession of New Orleans fixes the sentence. . . . From that moment, we must marry ourselves to the British fleet and nation. . . . Every eye in the United States is now fixed on this affair in Louisiana. Perhaps nothing since the Revolutionary War has produced more uneasy sensations through the body of the nation. (Ambrose 13)*

Unfortunately for Napoleon, he was forced to abandon his intention of reasserting France's presence in the western hemisphere. Costly military engagements in the Caribbean had drained much-needed resources, there were doubts about the French navy's ability to control lands so far away, and French officials feared that a rising population in the United States would make it difficult for France to hold back American pioneers on the western frontier.

Additionally, Napoleon had shifted his focus to European conquests and was aware of the infusion of cash that such *enterprises* would require. Accordingly, Napoleon shocked Livingston and Monroe by making a *counteroffer* to sell the United States not only New Orleans, but the entire Louisiana Territory (Stief).

Despite the fact that Livingston and Monroe had not been authorized by Jefferson to make this sort of deal, they seized the opportunity of a lifetime. Napoleon initially offered to sell the entire Louisiana territory to the United States for $22.5 million. However, Livingston and Monroe shrewdly negotiated the price down to $15 million. The treaty was ratified by Napoleon on May 1, 1803, thus completing one of the greatest real estate deals in world history. Jefferson, however, did not learn of the Purchase until July 3, upon which he promptly fed the news to the *National Intelligencer* (a Washington, D.C., newspaper). Fittingly, the story pronounced July 4 a day of "widespread joy of millions at an event which history will record among the most splendid in our *annals*" (Ambrose 14).

THE EXPEDITION

Jefferson had made three attempts, dating back almost 20 years prior to Lewis and Clark's journey, to organize American expeditions to find the Northwest Passage. In 1783, he approached revolutionary war hero George Rogers Clark (brother of William Clark) to lead an expedition; however, plans never solidified. Three years later, Jefferson met John Ledyard, who was from Connecticut. Ledyard had grand ideas of achieving fame and fortune by being the first to cross the North American continent. Ledyard presented a novel proposal that involved starting the trip in Russia, then crossing to Alaska, and from Alaska walking back to the Mississippi. Ledyard was able to launch his expedition; however, he never made it out of Siberia, as Catherine the Great had him arrested. In 1793, *botanist* Andre Michaux was commissioned by the American Philosophical Society, whose membership included both Thomas Jefferson (then secretary of state) and George Washington, to "seek for and pursue that route which shall form the shortest and most convenient communication between the higher parts of the Missouri and the Pacific Oceans" (Duncan and Burns 8). Unfortunately, even with initial seed money donated by Washington and Jefferson themselves, only a pathetic sum was raised and Michaux's trip had to be aborted while he was still on the Ohio River.

By early 1803, however, Jefferson, now president, was able to convince Congress to fund an expedition that would be scientific in nature but that would yield commercial benefits for the United States. With a $2500 appropriation from Congress, in the spring of 1803, Jefferson appointed Meriwether Lewis and William Clark to lead what he called his *Corps* of Discovery. Lewis, who had served as the president's sole aide, had dreamed of exploring the lands west of the Mississippi. Lewis invited his close friend William Clark to serve as co-commander of the expedition. Jefferson endorsed Lewis's request to have Clark accompany the corps on the proposed expedition. Clark brought a different skillset and a different perspective to the table, as he had a stronger military background than Lewis and had experience interacting with Native Americans.

Jefferson's written order to Meriwether Lewis reads, "The object of your mission is to explore the Missouri River, and such principal stream of it, as by its course and communication with the waters of the Pacific Ocean . . . may offer the most direct and practicable water communication across this continent for the purposes of commerce" (Duncan and Burns 14). Speaking to the scientific side of the expedition, Jefferson communicated his desire for the corps to gather information about this territory specific to its geography, its plants and animals, its people and their habits, and its potential for the young republic (9).

Lewis and Clark paddled initially down the Ohio River and then up the Mississippi to the mouth of the muddy Missouri River. They spent months there preparing for what would become one of the most important expeditions in American history. They assembled a *corps* of over 40 men, some with military experience, others skilled as frontiersmen. They built three *keelboats* and purchased a large stock of supplies ranging from guns and knives to food and drugs, clothing, blankets, mosquito netting, tools, and navigation instruments. They also brought along a large collection of goods to be used for *bartering* with the Native Americans whom they would encounter.

Finally, on May 14, 1804, the Corps of Discovery launched from Camp Wood, just outside of St. Louis. They were about to embark on what was to be a 3,700-mile journey from the Mississippi River to the Pacific Ocean. They would travel by boat, on horseback, and on foot. Considering the *trials* and *tribulations* of this long and *arduous* trip, it was remarkable that they lost only one of their company, Charles Floyd, who died of an apparent appendicitis attack just two months after the start of their journey.

During the summer and fall of 1804 the group paddled and, using poles, often pulled themselves upstream, heading northwest on the Missouri River to Fort Mandan, a trading post near present-day Bismarck, North Dakota. It was at Fort Mandan that the corps elected to set up camp for their first winter, and it was in North Dakota that they eventually met a French fur trader named Toussaint Charbonneau and his Shoshone wife, Sacagawea. Charbonneau and Sacagawea would become their guides, with Sacagawea serving as translator when the expedition encountered Shoshone people. That winter Sacagawea gave birth to a baby boy, who became the youngest member of the group.

By May 1805, the *corps* had reached Montana and eventually met the Shoshone, who were skilled at *traversing* the mountains. For this leg of the adventure the men rode on horseback. Once over the mountains, the *corps* employed the use of canoe-like boats to navigate downriver to the mouth of the Columbia River where they built a fort, Fort Clatsop, and spent another winter. It was November 1805. They spent four months at Fort Clatsop. In March 1806, the band decided to head back to St. Louis. On September 23, 1805, Meriwether Lewis, William Clark, and the *Corps* of Discovery arrived at their starting point.

The expedition had covered over 7,500 miles and had taken 28 months from start to finish. Lewis and Clark are credited with opening a new frontier for fur trade, but more importantly, they provided remarkably detailed maps of this new American territory. Lewis and Clark paved the initial, *albeit* crude, pathway to the west, eventually linking the Atlantic to the Pacific.

Keywords and Terms

1. annals
2. arduous
3. bartering
4. botanist
5. ceded
6. corps
7. counteroffer
8. enterprises
9. keelboats

10. traversing

11. trials

12. tribulations

BIBLIOGRAPHY

Ambrose, Stephen. *The Mississippi and the Making of a Nation: From the Louisiana Purchase to Today.* Washington, D.C.: National Geographic Society, 2002.

Duncan, Dayton, and Ken Burns. *Lewis & Clark: The Journey of the Corps of Discovery.* New York: Alfred A. Knopf, 1997.

Kennedy, Roger. *Mr. Jefferson's Lost Cause.* New York: Oxford University Press, 2003.

Kukla, Jon. *A Wilderness So Immense: The Louisiana Purchase and the Destiny of America.* 1st ed. New York: Alfred A. Knopf, 2003.

Lewis, Meriwether, and William Clark. *The Lewis and Clark Journals: An American Epic of Discovery.* Lincoln: University of Nebraska, 2003.

Lewis, Meriwether, William Clark, and Anthony Brandt. *The Journals of Lewis and Clark, by Meriwether Lewis and William Clark; edited and abridged by Anthony Brandt.* Washington, D.C.: National Geographic Society, 2002.

Stief, Colin. "Louisiana Purchase—The History of the Louisiana Purchase." about.com.geography. about. com, 2012. March 17, 2012. <http://geography.about.com/od/historyofgeography/a/louisianapur cha.htm>.

14

Acquisition of New Lands—The Louisiana Purchase: Book 1

Title: *Sacagawea*
Author: Judith St. George
Grade/Age: ages 8 and up
ISBN: 9780399231612
NCSS Standards: 1,2,3,4,5,6,8

ANNOTATION

This book is a biography of Sacagawea from the time she was captured by the Minnetaree when Lewis and Clark left for home. Much of what we learn is taken from the journals of Lewis and Clark and various members of their Corps of Discovery. In this book we learn Sacagawea's inner thoughts and feelings and get a window into her journey. Sacagawea is "given her wings" in this story and we learn about her baby, Pomp. The reader also learns the contributions she makes to Lewis and Clark's expedition.

SUGGESTED VOCABULARY

arrogant, breechcloth, camas roots, cormorants, dugout canoes, Fort Mandan, keelboat, Minnetaree, parfleche, pipe, prisoner, sentry, Shoshone, Sioux Indians, tipi

BEFORE READING: PREPARING TO JUMP INTO THE BOOK

Who Were Lewis and Clark?

Students visit the website <http://lewis-clark.org/> and read about Lewis and Clark's expedition to prepare for reading the book. After reading this information, students prepare five questions about Sacagawea's journey and the role she played in the expedition by Lewis and Clark. Students write their questions on the Questions I Want Answered Handout in Figure 14.1. When students come to the answer, they write the answer and the page number on the form. If their questions are not answered, they can use those remaining questions for further research.

Questions I Want Answered Handout

Questions I have	Answers I found	Page number

Figure 14.1: Questions I Want Answered Handout

Reading a Children's Book

Read Davis Adler's *A Picture Book of Sacagawea*, illustrated by Dan Brown. Conduct a read aloud with students by first doing a picture walk with students. Show students various illustrated pages and require them to make predictions about how the illustrations and text might be related. Inform students that many children's books are historical fiction as well and aim to teach children about a historical event. Students should pay special attention to how the pictures and text are related, as they will become authors and illustrators after reading *Sacagawea* by Judith St. George.

Examining Maps

It might be helpful for students to examine the journey of Lewis and Clark before reading the book. In addition to the maps found in textbooks, an interactive map can be found at <http://www.pbs.org/lewisandclark/trailmap/index.html>.

Active Reading

Students read the story about Sacagawea's baby, Pomp, online at <http://pompstory.home.mindspring.com/>. Students use the Active Reading Handout in Figure 14.2 while reading. Students stop at the end of each page and write two predictions for the next page. Once the predictions or revised or confirmed, the students fill in the appropriate blank.

DURING READING: GUIDED DISCUSSION QUESTIONS

1. Describe the opening scene at the beginning of Chapter 1. What happens to the young girl? How does she feel? How would you feel?
2. Why do the Minnetaree name the young girl Sacagawea?
3. In what circumstance does Sacagawea find herself in Chapter 2?
4. Why do you think the men with Sacagawea call themselves the Corps of Discovery?
5. Why are the soldiers afraid of the Sioux Indians?
6. Sacagawea and the men will travel to the Great Waters. What do you think the Great Waters is?
7. Sacagawea gives birth to a baby boy on February 11, 1805. Describe how she feels.
8. The men get scurvy. What is it? What happens to them as a result?
9. What does Sacagawea do to keep the men healthy while traveling?
10. What does Sacagawea do to prove herself worthy to Lewis and Clark?
11. Describe Lewis. Describe Clark. Do you think you would like both of the men? Why or why not?
12. What does Clark call Sacagawea? Why?
13. Why do Lewis and Clark keep detailed journals of their travels?
14. Compare and contrast the men's treatment of bears versus Sacagawea's treatment of bears.
15. Why do Lewis and Clark rename all of the rivers they encounter on their journey?
16. Sacagawea becomes ill. Why do you think this is so? How does Lewis react? How does she eventually heal?

Active Reading Handout

Chapter #	Predictions	What really happened?
#1		
#2		
#3		
#4		
#5		
#6		

Figure 14.2: Active Reading Handout

17. Describe how Clark saves the lives of Sacagawea and her son.
18. What do the Shoshone Indians do to warn their people of danger?
19. What advice does Sacagawea give Lewis about making friends with the Indians?
20. What is the significance of camas roots?
21. Why do they brand the horses with Lewis's name?
22. Since the men are weak from hunger, illness, and travel, they do not make their boats properly. What is the consequence?
23. Why is the tipi important in Indian culture?
24. Why are the women Indians called Flat Heads? How does Sacagawea feel about this?
25. What role does the Columbia River play in Indian life?
26. Why does Sacagawea give Lewis and Clark her belt? How would you feel about this if you were her?
27. Describe the winter of 1805.
28. The explorers steal from Indians. How does Sacagawea react to this?
29. Describe Lewis's battle at the Great Falls.
30. Why does Clark want to take Pomp to St. Louis?
31. What does Sacagawea contribute to the journey and the men?
32. What does Sacagawea mean when she says she was "given her wings"?
33. If you could ask Sacagawea three questions, what would they be?
34. What do you think is Sacagawea's strongest quality? What do you see as her weakest quality?

AFTER READING: CONNECTING TO THE TEXT

Creating a Coin

Distribute, if possible, a copy of a dollar coin with Sacagawea on it. If you cannot find the coin, you can show a picture of the coin found at <http://sacagaweadollarguide.com/>. Students can work in small groups to create a coin for another character from the book, or they can create a new coin to commemorate Sacagawea. Students should be required to create a rough draft of the front and back of the coin on paper before creating it from other materials. Allow students to use any material they want to show their creativity with the project.

Writing a Short Film Script

Instruct students to write a movie script for the book *Sacagawea* by Judith St. George. There are many accounts of Sacagawea's life and the part she played in settling the west. Students first describe what they will portray in their short film script. The scripts cannot be more than half an hour long. Students will write and direct the short film using a video camera. Students should use the Script Rubric found in Figure 14.3 as a guide to writing the script. Classroom teachers and school librarians can use it as an assessment tool.

Pomp's Perspective

Students work in small groups to brainstorm what Pomp would say about his journey with his mother, father, and Lewis and Clark, if he were old enough to talk at the time of the journey. Students should then create a story book from Pomp's perspective. Each person in the group is responsible for contributing to the children's book in some fashion. The children's

Script Rubric

	4	3	2	1
Conventions	There are fewer than 2 errors in spelling, grammar, and punctuation.	There are 3–5 errors in spelling, grammar, and punctuation.	There are 6–8 errors in spelling, grammar, and punctuation.	There are 9 or more errors in spelling, grammar, and punctuation.
Length & Content	Script includes three chapters from the book in a succinct, effective manner.	Script includes three chapters from the book in a somewhat succinct and effective manner.	Script includes two chapters from the book in a somewhat succinct and effective manner.	Script includes one chapter from the book in a somewhat succinct and effective manner.
Format	Includes proper use of **ALL** of the following: • scene headings • dialogue • transitions • actions	Includes proper use of **MOST** of the following: • scene headings • dialogue • transitions • actions	Includes proper use of **SOME** of the following: • scene headings • dialogue • transitions • actions	Includes proper use of **ONE OR NONE** of the following: • scene headings • dialogue • transitions • actions
Autobiography	Includes innovative use of autobiographical elements.	Relevant autobiographical elements included.	Autobiographical material present, but relevance unclear.	Autobiographical elements not present.

TOTAL: _____

Figure 14.3: Script Rubric

books should be a minimum of 10 pages, have a cover that displays the authors and illustrators, include a copyright page, and be historically accurate. The purpose of the children's book is to educate a young audience about Pomp's journey with his family and Lewis and Clark. Students who do not consider themselves artists can use clipart if appropriate. Classroom teachers and school librarians can find a valuable rubric at <http://www.readwritethink.org/files/resources/lesson_images/lesson1022/GradingRubric.pdf>.

DIGGING INTO THE DATABASE

Journal Writing

Students read the journal entries written by Lewis and Clark found in the school library's history database. They then write journal entries from the point of view of Sacagawea after she returns from her journey with Lewis and Clark. Students should date their entries and ensure that they are historically accurate.

Louisiana Purchase

Students research additional information about the Louisiana Purchase in the school library's history database. After reading this information, lead a class discussion about how Sacagawea played a significant part in this historical event. The classroom teacher should take notes on the chalkboard or chart paper for additional subjects that arise during the course of the discussion that students can investigate for future research.

Sketching a Scene

Classroom teachers and/or school librarians show an illustration or photograph of Sacagawea or Lewis and Clark. Illustrations can be found in the school library's history database. Lead a class discussion about the illustration. Then, ask students to choose their five favorite scenes from the book. The classroom teacher or school librarian then puts all the scenes in a hat and allows each student to pick a scene to illustrate. After all students have illustrated their scenes, require students, as a whole class, to put the illustrations in chronological order. Display the illustrations in the classroom or library display case.

Creating a Vocabulary List

Students create a list of 20 vocabulary terms they learn from reading information pertaining to Sacagawea, Louis and Clark, and the Westward Expansion from the history database.

READ ALIKES

Sacajawea by Anna L. Waldo ISBN 9780380842933 (Young Adult/Adult)

Sacajawea by Joseph Bruchac ISBN 9780152064556 (Young Adult/Adult)

Sacajawea by Joyce Milton ISBN 9780448425399 (Ages 9–12)

Sacagawea: A Biography by April R. Summitt ISBN 9780313346286 (Young Adult/Adult)

Sacagawea: American Pathfinder (Childhood of Famous Americans) by Flora Warren Seymour ISBN 9780689714825 (Young Adult/Adult)

Sacagawea: Crossing the Continent with Lewis & Clark by Emma Carlson Berne ISBN 9781402768453 (Ages 9–12)

Sacagawea Speaks: Beyond the Shining Mountains with Lewis and Clark by Joyce Badgley Hunsaker ISBN 9781585920792 (Young Adult/Adult)

Sacajawea: The Journey West by Elaine Raphael and Don Bolognese ISBN 9780590478984 (Ages 9–12)

Streams to the River, River to the Sea by Scott O'Dell ISBN 9780618966424 (Young Adult/Adult)

Who Was Sacagawea? by Judith Bloom Fradin and Dennis Brindell Fradin ISBN 780448424859 (Young Adult/Adult)

15

Acquisition of New Lands—The Louisiana Purchase: Book 2

Title: *Bold Journey West with Lewis and Clark*
Author: Charles Bohner
Grade/Age: Ages 10 and up
ISBN: 9780618437184
NCSS Standards: 1,2,3,4,5,6,8

ANNOTATION

Readers follow Hugh McNeal's journey with Lewis and Clark through the Northwest Passage. Although little information is known about McNeal, the author makes the character come alive with this first-person narrative supported by journals and other accounts. The youngest member of the army tells the tale of his experience with the famous explorers.

SUGGESTED VOCABULARY

berth, brandish, buckskins, cantankerous, court-martialed, expedition, fantods, flabbergasted, flapdoodle, flaxen, forage, freshet, gauntlet, gunwale, harangue, highfalutin, homestead, keel-boat, larder, Louisiana Territory, marksman, mischief, ornery, papoose, perilous, pirogues, powwow, rheumatism, scoundrel, sentinels, sextant, stockade, tipi, thwart, tomahawks, treacherous

BEFORE READING: PREPARING TO JUMP INTO THE BOOK

Making a Tipi

Students work with a partner or in a small group to research the origins of tipis and create their own miniature tipi out of a variety of materials. Students can tie four twigs, approximately 12 inches in length, together with a string, placing the string about three inches from one end of the collection of twigs. Students then gently pull the twigs away from each other until they create the shape of a tipi. Next, students trace the outline of just one side of the tipi.

This outline will serve as the template for creating the tent. Next, students cut out the template and open up a large brown grocery paper bag along its seams. They then lay the template on the bag and trace the outline of the triangle. Students can then trace the triangle three more times side by side, making sure the long edges of each of the triangles touch. When they are finished, their drawings should appear as polygon-shaped fans. Students then cut the fans along the outside edges and use scissors to create circular doors on the bottom of one of the four triangles. Students can then decorate the tipi with crayons, markers, or paint.

Similes and Metaphors

Before reading, review with students the definition of similes and metaphors. Distribute the Simile and Metaphor Handout in Figure 15.1. While reading, students should identify a number of similes and metaphors in the text. Students should write down the simile or metaphor, what it means, and the page on which they found it. Allow students to make a simile/metaphor wall in the classroom or library media center. Each time students find a simile or metaphor, they can write it on an 8 1/2 x 11 sheet of paper with an original illustration. After reading, check which student has the most similes and/or metaphors on his or her paper and award a prize.

Finding Hugh

Students work in small groups or pairs to research Private Hugh McNeal. Students can use the internet and books from the library collection or the school library's history database. Challenge students to find out as much as they can about the young army private who was part of Lewis and Clark's expedition.

Shoshone Acrostic Poem

Students write an acrostic poem about the Shoshone Indian tribe after researching its origins, traditions, dress, and so on using the internet or the school library's history database.

DURING READING: GUIDED DISCUSSION QUESTIONS

1. Describe how the narrator feels on the opening pages of the book.
2. What is the setting of the book?
3. Describe the strangers on page 4. Who do you think they are?
4. With whom do you think the narrator was speaking in Chapter 1?
5. What is the Northwest Passage?
6. What does the Captain want with Hugh McNeal?
7. What will Hugh be paid for going with Captain Bissel?
8. How old is Hugh? Do you think he is too young to join the army? Why or why not?
9. What is the Corps of Discovery?
10. What does George Drewyer show Hugh that upsets him in Chapter 3? How would you react? How does Jack react?
11. Describe Captain Lewis from Hugh's perspective.
12. Why do you think Hugh and Jack disagree often?
13. What does Hugh mean when he says, "I had the map of Ireland on my face" on page 21?
14. Describe the exchange between Captain Lewis and Hugh in Chapter 4.
15. What does Captain Lewis buy in Pittsburgh? Why?

Simile and Metaphor Handout

Simile or Metaphor	What does it mean?	Page number	Is it a simile or metaphor?
Silent as a cemetery	Nobody was talking because they were scared. A cemetery is extremely quiet.	p. 31	Simile

Figure 15.1: Simile and Metaphor Handout

16. What does Charley mean on page 30 when he says, "We are rowing Captain Lewis to glory"?
17. Why do you think Hugh dreams of earthquakes? Do you think the author is using foreshadowing? Why or why not?
18. Describe Patrick Gass.
19. Why does Patrick's story in Chapter 5 scare Hugh? Describe what he says.
20. What is George Drewyer's job?
21. How much is a week's wage in 1808? Does that surprise you? Why or why not?
22. Explain why the men throw Hugh into the river in Chapter 7.
23. How many men are in the Corps of Discovery? How did it grow to be so large?
24. What is *The Experiment*?
25. Moses plans to desert. What does that mean? What do you think will be the consequences?
26. Describe the men's first encounter with Indians.
27. Why doesn't Hugh sleep his first night after meeting the Indians? Would you feel the same way? Why or why not?
28. What do you predict will happen to Moses when he leaves?
29. How is Moses punished for deserting? How does the Indian chief react to the punishment?
30. Describe the summer months for the troops.
31. What do the men do to ward off mosquitoes?
32. What happens when the Corps of Discovery meets the Indians in Chapter 13?
33. Describe what happens between Jack Newman and Captain Lewis.
34. Describe Carbonneau. Who is he? Describe Sacagawea. Who is she?
35. Why do Lewis and Clark want Sacagawea to travel with the Corps of Discovery?
36. Describe how Hugh hurts his finger in Chapter 15.
37. What special talent does George Drewyer have?
38. Describe Hugh's hunting trip with George. What happens to his gun?
39. Describe John Shields.
40. What is the Indian sign for friendship?
41. What does Sacagawea do for the Corps of Discovery in Chapter 18?
42. Describe the Shoshone Indians.
43. What does Hugh fondly remember about Sacagawea and her papoose?
44. What obstacles do the men face in the mountains?
45. What happens to Hugh's horse?
46. Describe how the men feel when they see the Pacific Ocean. How would you react?
47. Did your view of Captain Lewis and Captain Clark change while reading the story? Explain.
48. How does Captain Lewis die?

AFTER READING: CONNECTING TO THE TEXT

Compare and Contrast Lewis and Clark

Using the Compare and Contrast Graphic Organizer in Figure I.5 found in the Introduction, students compare and contrast Lewis and Clark. Students must use examples from the text to support their claims.

Preparing for the Expedition

Students work in small groups to brainstorm a list of items Lewis and Clark may have taken on their expedition. Next, ask students to put their items into categories using the Expedition Graphic Organizer found in Figure 15.2. Categories might include, but are not limited to:

- Tools and instruments
- Camp supplies
- Clothing
- Arms and ammunition
- Medicine and medical supplies
- Types of books
- Gifts for Indians

The class should come together and share their list explaining why items are on their list. Next, share the information at <http://www.pbs.org/lewisandclark/inside/equip.html> and allow students to view the list of items and compare that list to their own. Ask students to answer the following questions:

1. What is on the Equip an Expedition list that is not on your list?
2. What items do you still think they would need after reading the novel?
3. Did they forget anything that you would have included?
4. How does this list differ from the list that might be created today?

Examining Journal Entries

Classroom teachers and/or school librarians can aid students in examining the journal entries of Lewis and Clark at <http://www.pbs.org/lewisandclark/archive/idx_jou.html>.

Email from Lewis and Clark

Lewis and Clark did not communicate via email, but they did use journals. After exploring the journal entries of the two men, students write an email from either Lewis or Clark to Sacagawea. What would he say? How would he treat her, and what language would he use to communicate his ideas? Students can use the Email Template in Figure 15.3 to write the entry.

DIGGING INTO THE DATABASE

Louisiana Purchase

Students read information about the Louisiana Purchase selected by the classroom teacher or school librarian. Information can be found in the school library's history database. Students then summarize the information using the Sum It Up worksheet at <http://www.reading quest.org/pdf/sumitup.pdf>. Classroom teachers or school librarians then have a class discussion about what role Lewis and Clark played.

Graphic Organizer

Figure 15.2: Graphic Organizer

Email Template

To: _____

From: _____

Cc:_____

Bcc: _____

Subject: _____

Figure 15.3: Email Template

Making the Trade

Students make a list of types of items that Lewis and Clark traded with the Indians during their expedition. Students should make a list of items they remember from the text and then begin researching using the database. A class discussion about the importance of trade and the part that bartering played during the era of Lewis and Clark should be explored.

How It Ended Debate

Using the school library's history database, students investigate how Lewis died, including the rumors surrounding his death. Ask students to engage in a debate, one side believing that Lewis died as a hero, one side believing he did not. Students can use the database as a resource to prepare for the debate.

Obituary Writing

Students visit the school library's history database and investigate one of the characters in the book. Students then write an obituary for that particular historical figure. Students might want to consider one of the following: Lewis, Clark, Sacagawea, Charbonneau, Jefferson, or Hugh McNeal. Once students finish their obituaries, they can type them using a word processing program and post their work on the school website or other secure site. Allow students to share their work in class as well.

READ ALIKES

Arundel by Kenneth Roberts ISBN 9780892723645 (Young Adult/Adult)

Burr by Gore Vidal ISBN 9780375708732 (Young Adult/Adult)

Drums by James Boyd ISBN 9780766194618 (Young Adult/Adult)

The Fighting Ground by Avi ISBN 9780064401852 (Young Adult/Adult)

Guns for General Washington: A Story of the American Revolution by Seymour Reit ISBN 9780152164355 (Ages 9–12)

The Hessian by Howard Fast ISBN 9781563246012 (Young Adult/Adult)

Oliver Wiswell by Kenneth Roberts ISBN 9781153523332 (Young Adult/Adult)

Rabble in Arms by Kenneth Roberts ISBN 9780892723867 (Young Adult/Adult)

Ruffles and Drums by Betty Cavanna ISBN 9780816712670 (Ages 9–12)

Time Enough for Drums by Ann Rinaldi ISBN 9780440228509 (Young Adult/Adult)

Author Index

Title Index

About the Authors

CARIANNE BERNADOWSKI, Ph.D., is an associate professor of elementary education in the Department of Education and Social Sciences at Robert Morris University. She has taught elementary, secondary, and college students for the past 15 years. She holds a Ph.D. from the University of Pittsburgh, an M.A. in reading education from Slippery Rock University of Pennsylvania, and a B.A. in journalism and communications/secondary education from Point Park College. Dr. Bernadowski has written three books published by Linworth Publishing— *Teaching with Books That Heal: Authentic Literature and Literacy Strategies to Help Children Cope with Everyday Problems* (with Patricia Kolenick), *Research-Based Reading Strategies in the Library for Adolescent Learners* (with Patricia Kolenick), and *Using the Coretta Scott King Award Winners to Teach Literacy Skills to Adolescents*—as well as *Teaching Historical Fiction with Ready-Made Literature Circles for Secondary Readers* (Libraries Unlimited).

She has authored several articles for *Library Media Connection, Teaching K-8, PA Reads, The Reading Professor, Middle Ground*, and *Teaching Tolerance*. She also serves as an educational consultant in the area of literacy education for school districts.

ROBERT DEL GRECO, Ed.D., is an assistant professor of elementary education and instructional leadership and management in the School of Education and Social Sciences at Robert Morris University. He was an elementary and middle school teacher for 14 years before becoming an elementary school principal (for 15 years) and eventually superintendent of schools (for 5 years). During his years as an elementary administrator, Dr. Del Greco served as principal of two Blue Ribbon schools, one state ranked and one nationally recognized. Dr. Del Greco holds an Ed.D. in administrative and policy studies, an M.Ed. in higher education, and a B.S. in elementary education, all from the University of Pittsburgh. He earned his principal certification and superintendent's letter of eligibility from Youngstown State University.

PATRICIA L. KOLENCIK, Ed.D., is an associate professor in the Teacher Education Department at Clarion University of Pennsylvania. Prior to teaching at Clarion University, she was a high school librarian for 27 years. She holds a doctorate in education from the University of Pittsburgh, an M.A. from the University of Alabama, Tuscaloosa, and a B.S. Ed. from Edinboro University of Pennsylvania. Dr. Kolencik has authored numerous articles for various scholarly and professional journals, including *Library Media Connection*. She is the co-author of Linworth's *Teaching with Books That Heal: Using Authentic Literature and Literacy Strategies to Help Children Cope with Everyday Problems* (with Carianne Bernadowski) and *Research-Based Reading Strategies in the Library for Adolescent Learners* (with Carianne Bernadowski).

CPSIA information can be obtained at www.ICGtesting.com
Printed in the USA
LVOW09s0608120214

373368LV00006B/52/P